About the Author

Christopher's appetite for science fiction is rooted in the wild and the zany. His drive for writing is anchored in his fascination with other peoples' lives, as well as his own. Tapping into societal issues while leaving room to veer off into nourishing bursts of escapism, Christopher seeks to thrill us, delight us, and dare us to question our own inner voices. He enjoys writing poetry, playing video games, daydreaming, gardening, foreign languages and cultures, and emerging technologies.

Runsdeep

Christopher Lee Scoville

Runsdeep

Olympia Publishers
London

www.olympiapublishers.com
OLYMPIA PAPERBACK EDITION

A CIP catalogue record for this title is available from the British Library.

ISBN: 978-1-80439-256-0

This is a work of fiction.
Names, characters, places and incidents originate from the writer's imagination. Any resemblance to actual persons, living or dead, is purely coincidental.

First Published in 2023

Olympia Publishers
Tallis House
2 Tallis Street
London
EC4Y 0AB

Printed in Great Britain

Dedication

For Ivy, for Cora, and for planet Earth.

Acknowledgements

My very special thanks to Katie Kaufman, whose feedback and notes have been essential to my writing and to this book. I also want to thank my wife, Ivy, as well as all my supporters, critics, and friends.

One

On December 3rd of the year 2051, Eric Sommerson wanted to die.

Not forever, that is. He would only do so intentionally, he decided, if he could come back to life. *If only it could be temporary,* he thought, like putting on a pair of slippers, or rather, like taking them off. This was his simplest of wishes, at least it seemed simple to him – to cross the veil long enough to see what else existed beyond his apartment and the end of his twelve-hour shift at the pizza crust factory. The oppressive boredom he experienced in that place gave him horrendous ennui, so slipping into the spirit world sounded like precisely the break in monotony he needed.

Eric's days varied painfully little. The sun would rise, it would set, and day by dreary day, he saw less of a difference between Endless Crusts Pizza Crust Factory and the rest of his life. His bed was a springboard to the bathroom. The bathroom was just another station from which to depart for the streets of Los Angeles. The streets in turn acted as a brutally efficient funnel through which he was hastened by forces beyond his control down into the machine. The machine used him up as fuel before spewing him out at the top, exhausted, to begin the process anew.

The elephant-sized machine that Eric manned was for mixing and extruding. It was almost fully automated. His solitary role was to visually monitor the slow churning of powdered,

11

ghost-white dough, make sure none of it overflowed, and to ensure that it flowed at a constant rate. The hours and pay were enough to afford Eric's pricey videogame habit. But during his twelve-hour shifts he would daydream about walking straight out the factory doors and down some random street he'd never walked on before.

The rare moments when the tiresome dullness of the factory gave way to a brief meditative state, Eric would have visions of blowing up space marauders with his grenade launcher, impressing a woman of royalty before whisking her away to safety, and other absurd, warlike, and fantastical scenarios. Then his line supervisor would shout at him to snap out of it, and it was back to reality – cold mechanisms of reality, churning the dough, woefully exuding crust after crust.

It wouldn't have been so bad, Eric thought, if he had a few friends who he could have fun with and relate to. Unfortunately, being an adult was proving to be the continuation that his B-series sitcom of a life did not ask for. This season kicked off with all the other machinists laughing at Eric when he tried to strike up a conversation and his voice squeaked. As if it were some plan cooked up in Hell to torture him, time slowed down as the whole room bawled out in laughter and made their jokes about Eric still going through puberty at twenty years old. Feeling in pain and alone, and realizing that no one was rushing to defend him, Eric melted on the spot and retreated from the break room to the Otto station outside, where he sobbed and screamed silently into his knuckles.

He thought about quitting then, calling an Otto and driving off without looking back. Accept defeat. How could he face the humiliation? There was the slightest trace of hope in his memory, someone's words as he ran away from the joking machinists, saying, "Oh, leave him alone!"

Down in the sub garage beneath the factory, there was little to no traffic at the Otto station between ten a.m. and six p.m. Decades-old mouse-sized robots had kept the rats and other pests away. It occurred to Eric while he was choking down his sour tears that he felt both embraced and isolated by the disembodied commercial jingle that pervaded the station. The tune was distinctly mellow with a bluesy saxophone. Every few minutes, the music volume would dampen, and a deep, sultry, masculine voice would sigh:

E n j o y t h e f i n e r t h i n g s . D r i n k S u l v e r .

Pale, chalk-white walls smooth and uniform as printer paper contained benches and ceilings of the same white, outlined with splashes of colorful poster ads. The place had its appeal, a silly fact which in itself further aggravated Eric.

Maybe I should shrug it off, he thought. *No – I have to shrug it off.*

It wouldn't be easy to do. In moments of desperation like this, knowing he was such a disappointment to his father made everything hurt all the more. Competition amongst the Sommersons was generations in the making, and this included competition in profession and business. Having his one and only son be a factory worker drew undesirable remarks from Mr. Sommerson's brothers, who thought the work beneath one of their own. Eric remembered how his dad used to urge him to stand up for himself, to not let people walk all over him.

Eric inhaled deeply, gathered himself, and went back to work.

The rest of the day went as expected. There was the occasional snicker whenever Eric walked past his coworkers. The sting had dulled, and by end of his shift he felt bolder and stronger. Soon he would switch on his game console and get back to what he did best. Then his wrist phone rang.

The Otto that was driving him home, like almost every car in operation on the United States VGPS grid, was always in self-driving mode. As of the passing of the Safer Pedestrians Act in September of 2048, switching out of self-driving mode was only allowed in cities and counties with populations less than a hundred thousand. Larger cities could enter manual-driving mode a limited number of times per month, but this freedom was rapidly being phased out. Exceeding the limit would disable your vehicle. Eric often wondered how such technology could exist yet somehow it was worth paying him to stare at pizza dough for twelve hours a day.

He answered the call with a pre-programmed hand gesture. The sincere chime of his mother's voice traveled in pristine quality through the speakers of the car.

"Hello, sweetie. How was work today?"

"It was fine. You usually don't call until I get home. What's up?"

"Your father and I would like to see you today. Can you update your route and stop over before you head home?"

Eric eyed his car's translucent yellow icon on the 3D holo-display as it traversed Pasadena. His apartment and electronic entertainment haven was twenty minutes away, while his parents' house would be at least an hour away, unless he took the hyperloop, and for that he'd have to cough up some cash. He hesitated to answer.

"No, I'm not going to give it away! Not completely!" Eric could hear his mother hushing his father, who pestered her in the background. "We have something for you," she returned to addressing Eric. "Something to show our appreciation for all your hard work!"

The little yellow icon started looking friendlier to Eric, and the distance to his parents a little closer. He wondered what the present could be.

"I'm on it. I'll be right over."

"I'll tell your father! We look forward to seeing you!"

Eric ended the call with a descending gesture, then flipped open his hyperloop app. It felt like a punch to the gut when he hit the PURCHASE button. Ten bucks wasn't a lot to spend to cut a two-hour trip down to twenty minutes, but in the last month Eric had bought a few more videogames than necessary. The Otto responded instantaneously to his trip update with a shimmy that preceded a lane change, highway exit, and entry into a long, gray tunnel. The tunnel was lined with glowing rings that zipped by in a blur of lavender.

Eric took in the view with a sigh while his Otto sped along the winding course of tracks that ran between the rain-stained columns of occasional overpasses. The tracks eventually brought Eric into a hyperloop pod. Cylindrical carrier pods like these could transport up to five Ottos at a time. After being whisked onto one of innumerable launch pads, Eric's pod accelerated just gradually enough to make the launch nigh imperceptible as it quickly attained a speed of three hundred miles per hour.

Eric watched the lavender rings zoom past faster and faster. When the pod reached close to four hundred miles per hour, the rings all blurred together like the words on a spinning tire.

Eric's childhood home had changed a lot over the years, but it was still humungous. The size of the place filled him with awe as a kid, but these days it made an already difficult visit even more uncomfortable. His mom was already opening the door, flanked by exquisitely ornate windows, by the time Eric reached the top of the prominent granite stairway. An elaborate pediment, the sole feature of the place that had remained unchanged since his childhood, bore the family's coat of arms overhead. The insignia depicted two blue lions with fancily styled manes flanking a red dragon head.

Eric's mother Vivian had a passion for keeping up with the latest trends in fashion and décor. A craze in Jakarta had gone pandemic, so naturally she was wearing a clear scarf that looked like plastic but felt like silk, matching a pair of long, spiky, turquoise earrings and black bracelets – *NADJANI's* winter line this season. She greeted him with the same exuberance as always, as though he'd just come back from some great odyssey.

"*There* you are! *So* glad you could make it. You're such a busy *man* these days!"

Vivian hurried her son into the house, hands clasped to his shoulders as she conducted him through the foyer, down a hallway, and straight to the living room to see his father. Mr. Sommerson was smiling in that way Eric knew could not be trusted. Of course, he could never be sure if his dad was genuinely happy to see him, or if he was dying to use the latest zinger he had up his sleeve.

"Hey, kiddo! Merry Christmas!"

"It isn't Christmas yet, Dad," Eric replied, a little annoyed.

"Well, for somebody, Christmas came early this year."

He guided Eric's attention with a nod.

Eric looked back to see his mother standing by the skyscraper Christmas tree, next to a glistening present in green wrapping paper that was taller than she was. Its shape was that of a Roman column. The gold trim that abundantly adorned most of the furniture and picture frames in the living room mirrored the soft shine of Vivian's hair.

"We'll have the movers ship it to your house tomorrow."

"Ship what?" Eric asked.

"Open it!" His parents both urged, his mother more so, his father less.

Should I try shaking it around and guessing what's inside? Eric decided against this, and instead set straight to ripping up the wrapping paper in a semi-neat, semi-chaotic fashion, grabbing at folds where he could find them.

Mr. and Mrs. Sommerson held each other in a sidearm embrace. They loved their son dearly. He was their only son, their only child, and always would be, and he didn't have to be successful to earn that place. Sure, they had wanted him to work the docks or go to college, but for whatever reason he chose not to. They knew he had his priorities. He made his intentions very clear from the time he was a freshman in high school. He didn't want a lot of pressure at work or to work a "hard job", but beyond that, he didn't really know what he wanted to do, and he wasn't much interested in deciding either way. Eric had found a decent job all the same though, for ample pay and even some decent benefits.

When Eric pulled away the last layer of shiny, metallic green paper and saw the logo stamped on the box underneath, he felt something akin to the chakras in his belly shooting straight up into the sky, threatening to pull him up past the clouds. The smile of all his childhood Christmases returned to his face for the first time in years. The VirtuaHelm™. It was the VirtuaHelm™!

Generations of video gamers had long dreamt about what the VirtuaHelm™ was to become. When the first ads started hitting the feeds and the last bastion of cable networks, people said that it was going to change the world similarly to how the smartphone did in the 2010s. It was still very new technology, only four months old. The various directions in which the nations of the world would eventually take it could only be guessed. Essentially a gaming station that allowed the user to completely immerse themselves in a virtual world, the machine consisted of three parts: helmet, station, and The Interface.

Eric stared at the magical, invisible cord depicted on the box that represented The Interface – a phenomenon belonging to a spooky, new realm of science. Whatever it was, it allowed the mind to connect to the network via some sort of incorruptible tether that manifested itself on the subatomic level. The science behind it all was too daunting for Eric to ever really want to learn. He did know that subatomic particles could be manipulated to form billions of lithe paths of data exchange. The result was a virtual world that was a lot like our own, though one with reduced graphics.

Eric turned back to face his parents feeling woozy in the head. This game system must have cost ten, maybe fifteen thousand dollars, depending on the model. Without bothering to finish removing the wrapping paper, he rushed over to hug them fiercely. Sure, they were very wealthy, and it was no hard thing for them to have done, but that wasn't the point. The unexpected gesture reassured Eric of their love for him, a realization that instantly melted away his recent ideations of suicide.

"Now you'll have something to look forward to at the end of the day!" Mr. Sommerson said. He meant well, but Mrs. Sommerson still gave his shoulder a disciplinary swat. Normally this sort of comment would have put Eric off, but he was too transfixed by the idea of logging into the Virtua world. His father couldn't have been more right.

The last day of the week unfolded exactly as Eric had foreseen it at his parents' house. Monday oozed by like the dough that so demanded his attention from morning 'til evening. A nightmare he'd had after leaving his parents' the night before still lingered in his thoughts. He had been surrounded by some awful white stuff. It was sticky, spreading, and it was suffocating him. Quickly realizing the truth, Eric whimpered and tried helplessly to punch his way free of the oppressive mush.

Back in his waking life, Eric glared at the churning white pizza dough, unnerved that the mindless, yeasty mishmash now pursued him in his dreams. *Clearly the dough does not move*, he thought – *the dough is moved*. Driven from one point to the next by the automated powers of the universe around it, making no assertions of its own, powerless, weak, a featureless eggshell-white blob, a pulp, nothing, only to be eaten in the end.

His gaze fixed on the churning mush, Eric whispered to himself, "No."

Exiting through the main factory doors, Eric felt excited and anxious. He kept his elbows tightly tucked against the sides of his abdomen as if he were walking through a crowd because he hated his bony elbows and how the wind reminded him of their gracile contour. Feeling the penetration of a slippery breeze, he mashed his elbows in even harder.

Several of the other workers were walking hand-in-hand with obvious partners, others with obvious spouses. Eric again felt a chill in the gap between his body and his elbows and cursed whoever designed buildings these days with the doors so far away from the pick-up area. Then he supposed it could have been an older building. *Whatever. Stupid design,* he thought. A five-minute walk later and he was stepping into his Otto, the automated transport service provided to workers by the factory.

Once inside the gaunt, hard-edged automobile resembling a silver-painted pinewood derby car, Eric commanded the AI to turn on the heat. A warm gust of air gradually increased in intensity, calibrated according to sensor readings of his vitals. The matte gray Otto departed the factory park and set off into the city.

Turning his head to window-gaze, Eric caught sight of a graffitied reproduction of the flag of the California Republic. The building on which the flag had been painted was broad and distant, allowing Eric a considerably long moment to observe the graffiti, which was masterfully done. The bear itself was not depicted in its typical profile, but had its head reared toward the viewer, its mane a flurried rainbow mix of colors. The tie-dyed beast retained its ferocity, and its wild eyes appeared to proclaim something unshakable.

The mural disappeared behind a series of buildings. Eric smiled.

Eric had read that, when first donning the game helmet and entering the Virtua world, you had to register your identity, then create your character or avatar, which could be a 3D model of your actual body (sans erotica, mind you, at least for the time being while Congress and the Supreme Court debated the matter) or a model of your own design. Eric envisioned having blond instead of black hair, being taller, maybe having different eyes, a different face. He could be anyone! Anything! And the games that awaited were bound to blow anything he had ever played out of the water.

In the commercials Eric had seen, when a player logs in, they are mentally transported to another world until they log out. The floor of the game station would move with such rapidity and responsiveness that the player could roll around, jump, do anything they would do in real life, all while remaining within the confines of the station, the walls of which were imaginary and tracked by sensors. Slippery surfaces were among the many features that the track could simulate, including any irregular surface or terrain one could possibly imagine. Anyone from a few decades back would have mistaken this track system for magic in the way it could morph and bend to match the player's virtual reality.

VirtuaHelm™ players would be alerted to any foreign presence or sounds in the area around the station. The machine was to be the shining achievement of videogame designers, with a dizzying variety of games to play and clubs to frequent. Eric's parents thought it ironic that he desired a virtual form of socialization, while real socialization was something he was so averse to.

The speakers inside the Otto played the company's signature jingle upon arrival at his apartment complex, a series of four towers connected at their bases as well as by skywalks halfway to the top floor. Eric could see people strolling between the towers through the glass skywalk walls.

He exited the vehicle and ascended the main stairs of the Cerulean Tower, where his apartment was located on the thirty-fifth floor. Eric always figured that there was no special reason for the name 'Cerulean Tower'. Each tower had a name. Although the walls and ceilings throughout the building matched the name with their cerulean color, he felt sure this was just an excuse not to name the building something uninspiring like Tower A or Tower One. *That makes sense*, he thought.

One main hall, one front desk check-in, an elevator ride, and three hallways later, and Eric was standing in one of the skyways he had seen from the steps far below. Taking a moment to slow things down, he looked out through the glass walls and watched people arriving and departing from the building.

His parents supplemented his income so that he could afford to live in a building with government-level security, but also so that his less-than-gainful income wouldn't so drastically alter the lifestyle he was accustomed to. Mr. Sommerson had vowed several times that the arrangement would not last forever, and this always earned him a good swatting from Mrs. Sommerson. Eric chortled to himself when he remembered this. Then he started to wonder how he would design his Virtua character.

Should I use my normal appearance? Before he could ponder this further, he noticed a young woman some twenty paces down the skyway who was walking toward him. They made eye contact. Eric felt a familiar panic swelling in the back of his throat. Nothing had really changed since high school, least of all his trouble talking to women.

"Excuse me, have you seen a guy wearing a bright Hawaiian shirt or whatever around here?"

Eric knew the answer to the question, but for a second he only saw how drop-dead gorgeous the woman was. Her smell alone was distracting, a dizzying aroma that rendered him senseless.

"He might be… in the other skyway… on the other side… the other side of the building," Eric replied vacantly, his attempt to not sound like a weirdo a complete crash, or at least so he thought. Her face didn't change. She seemed to be considering his answer. Then, with a polite smile,

"Oh! Good idea! Why didn't I think of that?" The woman thanked Eric, who nodded and returned his gaze to the moving lights of the cityscape before him. He'd only started to think about what the character customization system would be like when a shriek pierced the air and made him jump. It was the woman again.

"*Eeeeee!* I was just on my way over to *find you-u-u!*" The woman laid the cuteness on thick and cuddled up to a tall, strong type with broad shoulders. His Hawaiian-print shirt looked ridiculous and completely out of place on him, Eric thought. The strongman smirked at her coolly. Eric longed to play it cool like that. Maybe being big made the guy calmer, more sure of himself. Not wanting to listen to the coos and affections of the happy couple any longer, he power-walked to his apartment door, room 3514. He wriggled his key card out of his pocket, swiped it, and disappeared quick as he could from the hallway.

Thompson's made the most tolerable microwave dinners out of all the brands Eric had tried. Eric saw zero appeal in cooking and cleaning after half a day spent babysitting pizza dough, so normally he would have thrown another frozen meal into the microwave.

Not tonight.

The movers had already assembled the gaming station in exchange for the extra moolah Mrs. Sommerson slipped them. After moving Eric's armchair and end table and hobbling them alongside his couch, the movers had situated the track system in one corner of the living room, appearing as little more than plain vinyl floor, black as night. Organized and neat by nature, Eric was immediately put off at the thought of a trillion little white specks sticking to the perfectly dark surface, but his fascination with the thin profile of the track distracted him.

The VirtuaHelm™'s designers had achieved the impossible

by fitting such a sophisticated omnidirectional track system within a profile that was as thin as a yoga mat. *Beautiful,* Eric thought, and *perfect* too. Riding the rare buzz he was feeling, he unboxed the Virtua helmet at an eager yet clinical pace. He didn't feel good very often any more, not like when he was younger, and he sorely missed his childhood because of this. Any first-job teenager could do what he did. His father had reminded him of that in the past, which hadn't felt good at all. Unsure of how to remedy the problem, unmotivated and uninspired as he was to do anything else, Eric donned the helmet and pressed the power button.

The shadow of the blank helmet screen opened up into a dim backlit gray, and for a moment Eric recalled how, in the past, virtual reality was achieved by users wearing gloves in addition to helmets. Since the Virtua helm linked wirelessly and noninvasively (as ruled in a court of law) to the human brain itself, no gloves or cerebral modifications were necessary. He gasped when the dim gray merged completely with his full field of vision and flourished into lush shades of green. Somewhere far in the distance of this green universe, which was quiet but for the calmest sounds of a string quartet, a door opened, and through it came a humanlike figure of reflective bluish hues. The quartet escalated to a crescendo when the figure turned to look at Eric and emoted enthusiastically with a wave.

"Welcome!" cried the little blue person, who then pushed off the door as if floating through a space station and landed nimbly in front of Eric. Only now did Eric look down at himself and see that his own body was blank as the gray screen had been. The shape and proportions didn't seem right either, so the model couldn't have been based off of his actual body. The friendly blue sprite was an NPC, or non-player character, Eric assumed. He felt a certain discomfort in his gut at the possibility of not being able to tell the difference between AI and a human once he was logged in.

"I'm Ty! I'll guide you through your first log-in. Please remove the Virtua helmet and turn off the gaming system if you are epileptic or have difficulty telling fantasy from reality. VirtuaHelm™ is not responsible for any accidents related to these conditions. Do you want to customize your appearance, or should we go with your real-life look?"

Eric hesitated. He knew this decision was coming, but that didn't make it any easier to decide. If he went with his own appearance, he would be missing out on the opportunity to step out of his skin. At the same time, there was something about the choice to look different that made his gut fight with his head.

"Have you made a decision yet?" Ty asked after some time, startling Eric. The young man decided to go with his gut.

"Let's just go with the way I look." He regretted it the moment he said the words. Then Ty asked if he was sure, which he regretted even more.

"Yeah... yeah I'm sure."

"Okay!" Ty floated over to a portal that blipped into existence ten paces behind Eric. It bore the minimal appearance of a glowing white rectangle.

"This doorway will take you into the VirtuaHelm™ Server. I'll pop up and let you know if I detect any odd activity in your home while you're away. Any abnormal sounds will be instantly fed through to you so that you can decide whether you want to eject from the Server. Ask me anytime if you want to define specific sounds to be alerted for. Are you ready to go?"

Eric looked down at his hands again. They were his own hands now, pale and skinny, though lacking significantly in

25

detail. Given the technological limitations of the time, this reduced level of graphics allowed for a more immersive experience for the other four senses, which involved a colossal amount of data. The programming of smells alone proved to be beyond difficult for programmers.

"No rush. Take your time."

Eric shook himself into focus. The whole quasi-corporeal projection into a virtual world thing was more unnerving than he expected. *These things are designed to have all kinds of failsafes. It'll be fine.* Nodding his head awkwardly at the AI sprite, Eric stepped through the portal and was pulled into something, somewhere, far away.

Two

There was a saying in the Sommerson family that Eric's dad was always quick to remind him of at family gatherings – *A man's got to have a dream.* Apparently, it was Eric's dream to babysit a robot that bakes pizza.

No, Mr. Sommerson never said that second part out loud, yet, in a way that perhaps Mr. Sommerson would never know, Eric was now very much dreaming a dream.

The first sensation he had was that of falling. Not a terrifying plummet, but a soft descent with gentle breezes that combed his hair. Five glistening bars slid into view as he fell through the blank whiteout. When prompted, Eric entered his full name and contact information on a luminous keyboard that popped into view. He then slid the rainbow of scales a restricted number of degrees in order to select his desired stats: defense, strength, speed, and charm. A higher charm level gave players a higher chance of convincing NPC's to trust them. Eric went heavy on the charm, just in case he needed to talk his way out of a bad situation. People were hard enough to reason with.

What Eric saw next filled his stomach with more lovely butterflies than the Great Monarch Migration. Contained within a transparent bubble, he floated high above an opulent plaza where people walked and loitered by the thousand. Activity could be seen to course through the colorful amalgamations of multiform buildings which, seen from above, were arranged as though a mosaic of latticework surrounding the square.

Ty appeared inside the bubble with Eric in a burst of dissipating sparks.

"Your name, IP, and identification have been registered, however you may assume any identity you wish, whether real or imaginary, as you engage in the VirtuaHelm™ experience. Welcome to the city of Prium! Start Game Plaza lies directly below, but I can take you anywhere in the city you'd like to go. Just this once! As soon as you touch the ground, you're on your own – no more spheroid nimbus for you. Got it?"

The masses of people were like nothing Eric had ever seen. Only the largest marches and protests in remembered history could compare. In a virtual world, troublemakers could be booted from the game in the blink of an eye, so there was no concern about crowd control or lack of space. People weren't actually breathing the same air or posing any threat to each other's lives, so security could remain subtle and unseen. The general din of speech below was tangible. Eric could feel it in the soles of his feet.

"Would you like to see a map?" Eric took a deep breath. Ty apologized, "I'm sorry! I didn't mean to rush you."

"That's okay…" Eric suddenly felt strange. "Are you a computer?"

"In a manner of speaking, no!" Ty replied with a feverishly impish grin. Eric supposed this was meant to be charming, but instead he was creeped out.

"Just take me to where people normally start out."

Ty's grin impossibly increased by a sliver, and with a snap, the spheroid teleported Eric to the center of the plaza, where a series of portals floated around a grand fountain, the center of which supported a statue that would change shape every so often. People lounged along the edge of the fountain, taking in the digital sun. Eric thought to set straight to friend-making and introducing himself, but he was too bashful. He remembered Ty, who had disappeared with another sprinkling of sparks, and wondered who in the crowds was human and who might be a robot.

Eric dodged a few glances and began to walk around the fountain, inspecting the portals as he went. The fountain-loungers weren't in a hurry to get anywhere, though they did appear mildly interested in the new arrivals who materialized on the scene one after the other, stepping apart from the same position in a fine spray of sparks in the manner of a surreal human fax machine.

Eric recoiled in confusion when out of nowhere one of the newcomers materialized at a running pace. It was a man in a dated suit and tie carrying a briefcase. The Suit scrambled in a manic hurry to locate the first idle individual he could. Finding him in an instant, he seized Eric by the shoulders and with urgent eyes desperately asked him.

"Have you seen a crowd of paparazzi come through here? Where did they go? Speak up!"

The frantic man jostled an irritated Eric, who demanded in reply, "What are you talking about?"

Rather than explaining himself, the Suit promptly released Eric and sprinted straight for the nearest portal, which he dove into head-first, briefcase cradled in his arms. Eric stood frozen for a brief, perplexed moment before shrugging and moving on.

Clueless as to the direction he should take, Eric wandered without any destination in mind. As far as he could tell, this place was no different than real life (or RL) in that there was nobody to tell you where to go. His mind lingered on this for a moment until he caught sight of a beautiful woman with wispy red hair in purple fatigues and a gray tank top. She was part of a train of human traffic that was funneling itself into one of the gates, of which Eric counted twenty. Too interested to ignore her, and, having interest in no other path, Eric joined the river of people as they waddled in their slowly converging delta.

A stout woman of regal posture in the purest white robes stood serenely behind a podium at the right side of a remarkable gate the sight of which arrested Eric's breath. The gate had the appearance of a liquid water surface that constantly undulated from the center outwards in concentric circles. The serene woman spoke down at everyone trudging through the gate, making eye contact with each of them.

"Enter all who seek a time of change. Come one, come all! The world will be brand-new to you on the other side, but forget not that you are everywhere you go! It is not a world without upheaval, but in it, you shall be reborn. It is a place where you shall rediscover yourself. Come one, come all. Enter!" She repeated the words time and time again using the same tone, which led Eric to believe she was an NPC. The closer Eric got, the more easily he could see the pixels of the Virtua world disintegrating and collapsing around the portal.

Eric locked eyes with the robed woman for the briefest moment before he marched into the undulating waves. Upon passing through, his avatar and the world around him dissolved into a swirling cascade of color, sound and sensation. The five senses blended into one. Not just Eric's senses, but everyone's, as if their consciousnesses were all whipped into a frosting. In a fleeting glance, Eric saw the red-haired woman in her purple fatigues before she, like everyone, became fluid in shape and essence. A series of images then appeared before Eric which he did not understand but would instantly forget. They all had to do with the red-haired woman, though were increasingly less significant, like one hundred increasingly removed lifetimes.

The beginnings of a forgotten question were rekindled in his mind when he came to and realized he was strolling on a city sidewalk. The whole place looked like Las Vegas meets the galaxy's biggest video arcade, with a nice retro feel, Eric thought – a nod to the dawn of the digital age.

Eric skidded to a halt. Purple Fatigues was standing in front of him.

"You got a problem, buddy?"

Eric felt like his tongue slipped into a knot. He could see that the red-haired woman had a slender face and an easy-going posture, though evidently not an easy-going tone.

"I was… you looked like you knew where you were going."

"Of course I do. I'm not an idiot. What about you?"

Eric clenched the back of his throat, felt his eyes sting and water.

"Hey, hey I'm sorry. Listen, I can be a real asshole sometimes," the woman consoled, reluctantly remorseful. *Do not cry. Do NOT cry,* Eric commanded himself.

"It's just that I'm new and don't have any friends who are online right now," Eric allowed, trying his best to keep his voice from breaking. The woman sized him up. She wasn't sure what to think.

"I'm meeting a few friends to play Cry of Obedience. You can come with. Funny, I wouldn't do this in RL. You seem nice. Try anything creepy though and I swear to fuck I will report you and get your ass kicked off the server."

Eric accepted this readily, "Okay."

Purple Fatigues resumed her determined march. Eric followed at a safe distance behind her until they came upon what looked like an elevator to nowhere. The higher up he looked, the elevator, crudely made of concrete, gradually became transparent before ending with empty sky. Walking through, they suddenly appeared three stories above where they were, on a round-bottomed bridge overlapped by dozens of others.

Everyone was on foot, as there were no vehicles in this place for now. The teleport booths seemed to be the sole method of travel. Eric wondered whether it was worth taking the risk to bother Purple Fatigues when she took a sharp turn into a queue block – that is, a building made of bricks that gave off a neon glow, where players could join specific games. Not wanting to come off as too eager, Eric sauntered into the neon pink queue block. A blinking electric blue sign above the entrance read *Cry of Obedience*.

The liftoff from the ground took Eric by such surprise that he went stiff as a board when a tall, muscular Asian man lifted him by his shirt and pinned him to the wall. Eric found it impossible to respond as the man glared up at him. The Muscleman spoke over one shoulder out the side of his mouth in the deep bass of a tuba,

"You got a tail, Liz." He narrowed an imposing set of eyes at Eric, "It's cute, but it doesn't look good on you."

"Yeah, I picked that up just now on the way over." Purple Fatigues appeared with an ability-boosting soda pop in one hand while the other hand rested on her heavy-duty utility belt. "You think *he* could do the job, Maxx?"

"I don't know," the pec muscle of his free arm bounced formidably, "I spotted him a mile away. I suppose he might make a good distraction."

Eric wriggled his way free of Maxx's grip and fell to the floor with a painless yet audible thud. Liz sipped her soda pop. The grape fizz was still tickling her tongue and cheeks when she asked Eric, "Well, do you think you can dodge about ten rocket launchers there, Mr. Uh…?"

Eric got to his feet. Maxx backed off. "Call me Er– *wait a second, no* – um, Errigo, yeah."

Muscleman Maxx leaned in and asked, "Well, can you?"

"Can I what?"

"Can you dodge ten rocket launchers at the same time?"

Ridiculous, Eric thought, but he wanted to make a good impression. A stocky individual in a fedora and sleeveless shirt sat at the soda bar, arms crossed, staring silently at him. Eric was about to speak when he noticed a fourth set of eyes being aimed at him, the two red eyes of an oversized albino ferret standing behind the soda bar, pouring itself a drink.

Eric forced the words out through an initial stutter, "I-I can shoot a rocket launcher if that's what you need. I'm level 187 on Rockets vs. Jumpers."

The albino ferret emptied the bubbly drink into its gullet. Eric could see now that its chest and arms were strapped with ammunition. Someone wanted to look the part. *These must be hardcore shooters,* he figured.

Red Eyes twitched her whiskers and spoke in a shrill cartoon voice, "Guess that means one of us will have to be the bait!"

"Are you volunteering?" Maxx really wanted to know.

"Candy isn't one to stick her neck out first. You know that, Maxx." Liz was sizing Eric up again, still trying to figure out what to make of him.

Eric, getting the impression that he was coming off as a weirdo, asked, "What kind of a mission are you guys trying to pull off?"

Liz nodded over at Stocky Fedora, "Sam here will explain. Lay it on him, Sam." Liz finished her soda bottle and handed it to Candy, who snatched it and winged backwards without looking. The bottle landed square in a bin with a broken clatter. Candy's blood-red eyes boggled and darted.

The creature, or rather the human that occupied the avatar, had a lot of energy, and spoke before Sam could begin, "Yeah, um, so we're a pretty big deal on this one C-o-O subserver, but we were recently challenged by these bigshots from Korea after we won last season's international tournament."

"We didn't actually win," interjected Maxx. "We just beat the Korean team in the semifinals. They call themselves Chrome Tigers. Lame nickname if you ask me, but they're super popular, so beating them was basically like winning in the eyes of the community. A crew has got to have a name that bewilders or threatens, not one that's appealing and makes you want to join."

"What's your guys' crew called?" Eric asked.

"Seahorse Mafia."

"Will you let Sam speak already?" Liz looked mean. It made Eric's heart flutter. She couldn't be messed with. She was a force, a steady, sturdy power.

Sam began, "Right. The name's Sam. I use the gender-neutral pronouns *xe, xyr, xem, xemself,* okay?" Sam removed what looked like a discrete, green glowstick from one of xyr pockets and used it to trace a floating box in the air. Upon connecting the last corner, the box lit up like a computer screen, and Sam opened a link on the desktop to play a silent montage of photos and articles related to the upcoming event. "So, Chrome Tigers challenged us the night after we beat them during the semis, then things got out of hand."

Sam slowed the video down and pointed to a graph that was being explained by a news anchor.

"Chrome Tiger followers started a betting war that went

34

pandemic, and before we knew it we were being targeted. It wasn't too bad at first. Managers and promoters tried to cut deals with us so they could cash in on our rise in popularity, but then we started running into rogue fixers who were trying to sabotage us. There's a lot riding on the match at this point. It's gotten so bad that we've had to change our appearance – hair color, makeup, species, anything. It only helps so much. Liz here is the only one who looks the same."

Eric wondered why only Liz had chosen her own appearance, just as he had. Sam's tattoo of a dragon coiled around a girthy bicep caught his eye as xe went on. The graphics of the tattoo were pixelated.

"A narrative switcheroo - let's throw these cocky chumps out of their little crow's nest before the competition even begins. If you ixnay someone outside of a subserver, they're booted off the Virtua server and into Limbo for twenty-four hours. That way, we win by default *and* by combat, once in the arena and once out of it."

Eric recalled a TV commercial depicting Limbo as a kind of virtual afterlife.

"Their crow's nest?" Eric asked. Liz stood up and fast-forwarded through Sam's video by dragging her finger along the progress bar. She paused on an image of a mammoth treehouse that overlooked a bustling valley of chatrooms, restaurants, and clubs. Eric marveled at how none of it was physically real, how it was all the Interface's signal broadcast into the synapses of each player's brain.

"Their hideout. They call it The Crow's Nest. Not sure why *Chrome Tigers* would hang out in a *crow's nest* but whatever."

"Why do you have it out for these guys so bad?" Eric needed a convincing reason. The action sounded exciting, and he was eager as ever to make friends, but he wasn't eager to make new enemies.

"They body-shamed Candy, and they gay-bashed Maxx," Liz spat the words. Suddenly Eric understood the crew's fierce intensity. As delicately as she could with one cushiony finger, Candy wiped away painful tears. Maxx flexed his whole body, lifted his head, unwilling to appear hurt for a single second, yet to Eric, this had the opposite effect. Seeing this, seeing Liz and her faraway look while Sam grew broody and looked down at xyr feet, Eric had his convincing reason.

"That's terrible. How could they do that?" He was genuinely confused.

"Yah," answered Liz curtly, annoyed. Eric figured he should probably quit talking. Releasing a brief, subdued sob, Candy cleared her throat and hoisted a rifle of tank-piercing caliber up onto one shoulder.

"Let's gore these nut sacks."

The Crow's Nest was bumping, but that didn't mean that the pregame party was unprotected. The foretold ten guards armed with rocket launchers stood watch over the property leading up to the enormous tree. The yard's aesthetic, inspired by the group's affinity for zombie trap music, was that of an elephant graveyard mixed with faded headstones and mausoleic architecture streaked with shriveled black vines. Joon-woo, the leader of Chrome Tigers, loved a good party the day before a competition, and tonight the Virtua wine kept flowing. Inebriation, fatigue, all states of mind and body were possible in the Virtua world, though not necessarily inevitable.

Eric remained as still as possible. The spice of autumnal evening dew and dead leaves filled his nostrils. Here, at the edge of this brave new proto-world, he caught his first glimpse of the desolate expanse known as the Outlands. Eric had read about the empty stretches of badland plains, how they went on forever. Sometimes people would form bands and roam the wastes just for the hell of it. Some would adjust their avatars to realistic settings that required the eating of Virtua food and drink in order to see how long they could survive. Rumors are that while most of these bands perish, some maintain their existences and save points using a system of separate characters and item trade flows.

Eric's nervous, vise-like grip clawed deeper into his rocket launcher when the first battle cry rang out. It was Candy, making a spectacle of herself. The reason for this was beyond Eric. *Why announce our presence? We could have gotten the jump on them.* He took aim and let fly his first projectile, which cruised just above its mark, sailing over the head of one shooter.

"Lower!" Liz cried before landing her own rocket square above another guard, causing boulders to fall and put him out of commission with a muted crunch. Sprinting on all fours, Candy hallooed at the sight of this before she was nearly blown to bits. A well-timed rocket had come zipping down from the treehouse, blowing a hole in the rock formation beneath her. Streams of partygoers began to spill out of the hideout.

Eric felt an alien thrill building in his chest as he heaved real breaths of real excitement. Luckily he perceived the accuracy of the next oncoming rocket in time to drop down into his ditch, although a traveling vendor on the street multiple blocks behind him, which was an NPC, perished a random and grotesque fate. Maxx roared in laughter at this.

Candy's new, long, agile body, combined with her stats, gave her the finesse needed to evade being vaporized by the volleys of ordnance. She was a quick one even before the transformation, including in RL, despite her weight, but now she was cooking with gas. When another barrage of rockets came streaming down, trailing plumes of smoke that rose like the lights on an equalizer display, Liz and Sam provided cover fire from the sides of a defensive boulder. They took turns firing in varying patterns. Their gunfire was deafening, but it was when the rockets hit the yard that auditory functions were interrupted for everyone on the property. Eric felt the change in wind direction and the lash of the expanding debris clouds that jacked up the equalizer display. A hunk of pixelated sod whapped him in the face while he tried to get eyes on his target. Eric spit dirt and rocks. Liz called, "We make our move in five… four…"

"Errigo!" Sam yelled, "You got us covered?"

The missile barrage intensified and focused on Candy as she approached the trunk of the great tree, weaving between mausoleums, knolls, and gnarly roots. The Chrome Tigers themselves had assembled inside the hideout.

Eric shouted back, "I'm unloading on the fort! Ready when you are!"

"… two… one…"

The Chrome Tigers barged out onto their deck that overlooked the graveyard in dramatic, debonair fashion. One had a pinstriped mohawk. The leader Joon-woo was dressed like a 00-agent in a nine-thousand-dollar suit, and the rest looked like the rave entourage that they were, bedecked in glow sticks and brand-name kicks of the highest digitalized quality.

Eric lined up his boom stick and fired. Joon-woo had just enough time to tear the sunglasses from his face and catch sight of the oncoming rocket. He screamed, "Get back ins–!"

The deck and all its decorations went up like a flaming Christmas tree. The rapid destruction increased into a crescendo of expanding rubble that filled the air and inflicted a temporary lag onto the graphics for everyone in the vicinity. Liz and Sam hooted like they'd just won the world tournament. Taking care to ensure their victory, Sam's sniper rounds dispatched the remaining baddies who pulled up the rear. Candy, having taken shelter in a faux well, was safe from any remaining guards' attempts to make her pay for her romp. At last, all fell quiet.

When the dust settled, Candy emerged from the well with a mischievous grin.

"You guys didn't disappoint. Didn't leave any leftovers for me though. A girl could be offended."

Liz kept her launcher mounted on one shoulder, ready to aim and shoot should another bogey arrive late to the party. Sam had no pity for Candy, and scolded her for not being content with nearly getting nullified.

"Always the big talker. You know, you won't be talking so big one of these days. What were you thinking? What happened to the signals? You dashed straight up to the front gate like you had a death wish."

Candy denied that she had acted recklessly, and the two bickered back and forth. Liz, satisfied that they were safe enough to take her eyes off the steadily burning hideout, flashed Eric a smile.

"They're always like this. It's adorable really."

A small crowd of curious passersby started to congregate near the gate that led out of town to the treehouse. This wasn't just any Sunday stroll though, i.e. Eric wasn't sunk into his couch at home beneath a TV dinner tray, learning about theories of dark matter. The immediate threat of their dispatched opponents could easily be followed by another shooting spree if any of the onlookers decided they were feeling froggy. The best time to act is when a fight has just ended. The survivors are fatigued, the spoils are fresh and often undefended.

One of the people in the crowd stood out to Eric. He was a slight man with russet brown hair and brown eyes who seemed less engaged than the others, yet somehow more interested. The man's eyes spelled something between fascination and confusion.

"Looks like we better get a move-on," Liz said before slapping Eric's wrist with a strip of light that promptly melted into him. "My contact info. We might need you on another mission. Get out of here and lay low. Later!"

Candy and Sam were already ahead of her, lifting up a manhole which would lead undoubtedly into the bowels of the city. The way Eric saw it, there were some places he wasn't sure he should go. Liz wanted them to split up for now anyways, and besides, he didn't want to overstay his welcome. He was feeling a delightful buzz. Unpacking the VirtuaHelm^{TM} was one thing, but the decent human interactions – albeit after an initial chokehold – had felt like his first warm bath in a year. Before Eric could make his getaway into a portal that led to some destination he was unfamiliar with, the peculiar brown-haired man cut him off with a casual saunter, his head hanging low as he chuckled in.

"You got it bad, don't you?"

"What do you mean?" Eric had a feeling he knew exactly what the stranger meant. The man's turtleneck and glasses made him look like a pupil at Hogwarts.

"The girl." He gave a reverse, upward nod. "You guys took out the Tiger gang. They've been ransacking the auction houses around here. You did people a favor. Doesn't hide the fact that you're head over heels though."

How does a guy respond to that? Most people would have probably told the dude to get a life, but Eric wasn't like most people.

"I just met those guys earlier today."

"Guys?" The stranger narrowed his eyes. "I saw one man, two women, and one weasel or something."

"Sam uses gender-neutral pronouns. I'm not sure if she, er– if Sam's a woman."

The stranger contorted his face in a way that Eric had trouble deciphering. He might have been thinking something like *yeah well, whatever you say.*

Russet Brown Hair started to walk off into the city, leaving with these words, "The name's Lester. Welcome to the party. Be careful who you make friends with around here."

Eric considered asking the stranger what he meant by that last part, but he was getting tired. He reached to the back of his head, and, recognizing this gesture, the Virtua server simultaneously severed The Interface. Eric woke up in his apartment, which was quiet as could be.

Three

Gavin Jacobson loved having Eric Sommerson around. The putz made him look good, superior. He could turn Eric into the butt of every joke. Nobody would ever tell him to knock it off either, not even when he cornered Eric in the breakroom and reminded him that he'd always be a loser. "That's all there is in the end," he had said, snidely giving Eric a taunting stare. "Winners and losers." See, there was an order to things in the world. Sometimes people like Eric needed to be reminded of that.

"You? You're going to keep working this shitty job the rest of your life, because there's always somebody who does. The winners are the ones who move up in life, while people like you sit at the bottom."

Gavin would have loved to sock him in the face. Not because he hated Eric, no. It wasn't anything personal. It was because Eric was an easy target – the same reason Gavin slugged every sissy he squared off with. Of course, Eric wouldn't have defended himself, and if he had, he would have just melted into a puddle in ten seconds anyway. It felt good to put him down, to remind him of his place. Eric wanted to cry, then to die, then to cry and then die again. Finally Gavin walked off, smug in his solid position of power over Eric, who couldn't wait for his shift to end.

A blank chat window occupied the screen of Eric's tablet for about an hour while he contemplated what to say in his message to Liz. He never was great with words. It was one of the things that constantly made him compare himself to Gavin, who had the gift of gab and was charismatic and well-liked by many. He decided at last that torturing himself was getting him nowhere and swiped the screen into sleep mode. If he couldn't say the right thing, he would do the right thing.

After driving an extra TV dinner into his belly so that he could commit to a longer gaming session, Eric strapped on the VR helmet and logged in, keeping his encounter with Ty the NPC brief. The digital sprite was fun, but there was a quest to be undertaken. *Nothing specific has to happen with Liz,* Eric told himself. He just wanted a friend. The fact that he couldn't get the image out of his head of her lush, scarlet hair being whipped around by the explosive winds in the previous day's firefight was an innocent bonus. He had done something right for a change too, and it paid off.

The city of Prium was as busy as the day before, with an uncountable abundance of people. Eric opened the lid of a trash can and looked inside. Bad graphics, but it was cool they went so far as to program in crumpled bits of newspapers that were actually published in the city, along with other faux detritus or discarded items like soda cans. Closing the lid, he was taken off-guard by a pop-up message that blipped into his field of vision. The small yellow text inside a black box read:

Liz87_Firefly: Hey we're not in Prium today. Find a portal to Izzna and tell me when you get to the beach.

A beach subserver sounded appealing to Eric. Optimism filled him while images of curvy beaches and Liz's curvy figure in a bikini filled him further still. He could handle work and Gavin and the peanut gallery if every now and then he could have a beach getaway. Finding the portal wouldn't be hard.

43

Prium and all its bright lights were just the beginning of the Server's potential. Street after colorful street, Eric ambled along. *You can walk however you want to here,* he thought. Back in RL, you have to look over your shoulder because anyone could be coming up from behind you. You have to fear hazards and death. Here, falling off a cliff will not end your life. A person cannot drown. Dying only ends the game or kicks you off the Server, depending on whether you're in the open world or on a subserver.

When Eric stood at the edge of the sidewalk and watched a stream of eight cars crash into the sides of several buildings and scream past him, it was exciting. He laughed when he saw them trying to drive each other off the road. None of it was real. People could do anything, and yet, not one bit of it, not a single act went unseen.

Monitors stood watch over every field of playable space. No one in the general public knew exactly how many there were. While the Server's administrators were more akin to social engineers than corporate masters, liability was an issue that they took very seriously, given that their bank accounts were at stake.

One Monitor named Terryl had a certain disdain for the demands of his bosses and his bosses' bosses, so he acted much less aggressively in his monitoring. A good Monitor could easily stay busy keeping an eye on the Server's activity, so hiding his reluctance wasn't a simple task. The restrictions on conversation were rules that he couldn't abide. Hate speech fell under free speech as far as Terryl was concerned. *It would be like making swear words illegal,* he thought as he glided through the air and panned his view of the world around him. Soon he would need to find a lawbreaker and issue them a warning, citation, or banishment order, depending on their number of previous infractions.

Halting his progress, Terryl zoomed and 'threw his ears' via trans-audio reception to monitor an interaction that was taking place atop a walk bridge that crossed a shimmery river with jagged yet strangely elegant graphics. He was about to begin his recording when the sound of a familiar voice startled him.

"Making the e-world safe for Big Brother's snowflake collective, I see," Lester chimed in with a gushing upstairs tone. His presence wasn't unwelcome, but it always put Terryl on edge.

"At least I get to work on the Server. Do you have any idea how fun it is to fly around like this? The whole universe is click-and-drag to me."

"There is no other more skilled at dragging and clicking than you, *T*," Lester praised Terryl facetiously. He had a habit of abbreviating people's names. "Speaking of, are you ready to put those skills of yours to a nobler use?"

Terryl didn't answer right away. Lester, a hacker, had made similar offers in the past, all of them tempting, but breaking protocol on his own time and for his own purposes was one thing. Collaborating with someone outside of administration entailed the possibility of a much more severe consequence.

Computerized stars twinkled overhead. Floating near the water of a wide river beneath an imposing Gothic drawbridge, Terryl couldn't help but wonder whether Lester was a racist, and whether being black was going to be a problem if Terryl decided to help him. After listening to his speeches and reading his anonymous essays, he couldn't deny that he liked the man's ideas, but you had to be careful. Racism wasn't dead in 2051. At last Terryl answered, "What do you have in mind?"

"There's a new kid in town. A new profile that just popped up yesterday. He's got the makings of somebody I can rely on." Terryl pursed his brow in confusion at this. Lester waved a

45

dismissive hand, "I'll bring you up to speed soon. Just be ready."
Lester departed with a crackle of static and pixels. Hacker
that he was, he could slip into the admin realm and play Monitor
for short periods of time before the Server's malware ID sweeps
could identify and locate him. This was one more reason for
Terryl not to completely trust him. It was impossible to know
what he was capable of. His ability to enter the admin realm at
will was itself a complete mystery, one that Terryl would have to
keep to himself for the time being until he could learn what the
man had in store for their mutual cause.

Sam read quietly while xe enjoyed the warmth of sunlight
without the radiation. Liz was sprawled out belly-up on her
gossamer, zany-patterned orange beach towel. Eric strolled up.
Maxx saw him coming first. Maxx always saw everything first.
A lump instantly formed in Eric's throat, as well as in another
region in RL, when he caught sight of Liz's body and her hair
swept free by the Izzna seaside air.

"You made it! That didn't take you very long." Liz was in a
much brighter, happier mood compared to when Eric first met
her, but she was still about three pegs below bubbly. Eric shifted
his posture as gracefully as he could and sat down on the bare
sand.

"Yeah, I got some directions from a group of RPG gamers.
They told me that I would love it here and that I just had to visit."

"Enjoying the view?" Maxx asked, noticing that Eric was
eyeing Liz's body a bit too obviously. Sam cleared xyr throat
uncomfortably. Candy wasn't paying attention. She was
sprawled out similarly to Liz on her own extra-long beach towel
to accommodate her long ferret body.

"What did you think of the esplanade?" Liz asked.

Eric broke free of his trance. "The what?"

"The flat seaside area with all the walking lanes and vantage points that you took to get here. Quite a sight, isn't it?"

"Yeah. Yeah it is. Very nice." Eric couldn't argue. Now if he could only think of something else to say…

"What would you say if I told you that the leader of the free world is going to log into the Server and give a speech at a volleyball tournament tonight?"

This, Eric thought, had to be a work of fiction. A sensational headline to get people to think that republican Yessica Li Lundgrasse was in touch with her *cool* side, which meant chillaxing with today's videogamers, who accounted for almost ninety percent of the population. What more extravagant yet unquestionable way to indicate that she was *cool* (or *on the drip* as the kids were calling it these days)? What wasn't on the drip was Lundgrasse's rumored homophobia. The evidence was clear enough.

"The United States needs now, more than ever, the guidance of our savior Jesus Christ," the president had said during her public speech announcing an upcoming push for new marital legislation, to the uproar of many. The supreme court had recently gotten a lot more conservative thanks to her too, and it was making for a – news flash – volatile political environment.

The remaining details were fuzzy or unimportant to Eric, whose politics were not exactly well-informed. The matter concerned the public's foresight. They knew, or thought they knew, what president Lundgrasse's next move was going to be. Many leftists and human rights activists feared that same-sex marriage would be somehow made illegal again.

"I guess a VR speech would be a smart move, politically speaking," Eric offered.

"Yah, it's not like everyone is tripping over themselves to applaud her parade." Maxx's muscles bulged out from his core and branched apart, wrapping his body in an intimidating suit of armor. "You didn't vote for that harpy, did you?"

Eric felt he could shrink down to the size of a pea beneath that angry glare. Sam dropped the magazine xe'd been reading. Xyr chest rose and fell sharply as xe heaved a sigh and interjected, "Leave the poor man alone, Muscles. Do you want him to walk away from his brand-new boat?"

Liz rolled up her own magazine and swatted Sam in the shoulder with it. Candy yawned and turned away from them. She had been motionless up until now.

"Shhhh!" Liz looked around to make sure nobody was listening. "We can't talk about it here." She looked at Eric, "Let's just say there's a sweet reward in it for you if you can help us pull off this next job."

Right, a job that we can't talk about here either, Eric figured when he thought to ask. Maxx persisted with his glare. Words at that moment had all the structural integrity of eggshells, so it only felt right to just agree and change the subject. He could always back out later, which he figured he would probably have to do. Something this secretive involving the president did not feel like the kind of field trip he wanted to go on.

"I'll help. What do we do in the meantime?"

Candy rolled over and laid her head on Sam's lap. Sam protested this in frustration, reminding Candy that xe didn't like people invading xyr personal space. Candy, to Sam's offense, neglected to apologize and instead rolled her long, furry neck over onto Liz's lap.

"We party, knucklehead!"

And party they did – watersport racing led by a socially

48

unhinged man named Fresno who lost his legs in a base-jumping accident and whose self-proclaimed purpose was to make people excited about life. Too manic to have slowed down or to have worked enough to save any money, Fresno explained that he couldn't afford the slick robotic legs that were available at a topnotch hospital not far away, so he darted around in an engineless wheelchair equipped with special, pump-up wheels that even let him scoot across the sand. He would officiate their races, declare the winners, and spray an endless supply of digital champagne onto everyone in descending order after they crossed the finish line. Rinse and repeat. Windsurfing was up after that, and Eric was forced to keep his own concerns in check when Fresno strapped his wheelchair to a waterboard and took to windsurfing with the rest of the partiers who had logged in from Mexico and Canada.

Then it dawned on Eric. Fresno could have chosen any form, yet he chose to remain in a wheelchair even on the Server. He wondered, *Why turn down a superhero's physique for a disability?* Then, more nearly, *If the VirtuaHelm^{TM} could let you be anything or anyone, why would you just be yourself?* The answer stared him in the face as he began to enter his question into a private message to send to Fresno's inbox. Seeing the face of the avatar Fresno had selected, Eric recalled that he had chosen to be himself as well.

Eric gave the windsurfing a try. Gliding across the water was a beautiful experience despite its noticeable CGI qualities. It was a leisurely break from the racing, which had lasted for over an hour. Maxx had been highly competitive the entire time. At one point Eric came gliding up alongside Fresno, who rode quietly across the water and gazed out at a digital sunset. He was so serene. Majestic, really. Long-haired, hippy eyes, free. He peeked at Eric with a knowing glance, "It's the calm before the storm, isn't it?" He smiled, still serene.

"What storm?" It was the last word Eric expected out of Fresno's mouth. Everything about the man appeared to be the opposite of a storm. The tranquil hippy let go with one hand and held on with the other, allowing himself to dangle closer to the water.

"You." His smile grew. Eric froze, and Fresno chuckled lightly in turn, "No worries, I'm in on the whole thing. Liz wanted me to fill you in. We can talk out here as long as we're not too loud. For some reason the graphical data communication between the water and the Server provides enough background noise when you're this far out. Admins will probably figure it out sooner or later."

From a distance, Liz gave Eric an approving nod. This assured him that Fresno was telling the truth. Content with this, he asked, "So what's the plan?"

"The target is, as you know, either famous or infamous depending on your persuasion." Fresno swooped over the top of a wave peak. "When she gives her big speech on the esplanade, there's going to be a fireworks display out here on the water. We're going to hijack one of the firework boats and turn the event into a real show. We can use the boat to blend in as we approach the esplanade, which is going to be under tight security to ensure the president's pleasant experience of the Server."

Eric was uneasy. He anticipated what Fresno would say next. "Then, while she's giving her speech, we're going bring those rocket launchers out of early retirement and send a message to the world: This is what the Server thinks of your Bible-thumping!"

"We won't be hurting the president, will we?"

"How could we? It's all virtual reality, my dude. No harm, no foul. It's all about the imagery. People see the burning esplanade, the wooden planks programmed to ignite just like real ones. Programmers will be too late to delete the effect. Sure, they'll get around to it quickly, but not before the president stands before the cameras against a backdrop of flames."

Now this did in fact make Eric smile, though it was pure Schadenfreude, an emotion for which he tended to scold himself. He didn't really understand the goings-on of the political world, but he didn't much see any harm in gay couples getting married either. What could the harm be? Not to mention the idea of an important societal figurehead having her grandiose plans so dashed made his heart jump. Maybe it was because he'd always been the little guy, the guy that finished last. If anybody else's definition mattered, he was essentially a loser, plain and simple – that's what he figured. Undiscernible and unnoticeable, at least until the day that Liz's crew asked him to dodge rockets. Knocking another big kahuna off her high horse would feel good. He knew it would.

Getting back to the beach was easy. They teleported. The Izzna subserver equipped players with bracelets that would meld with your wrist and allow you to save one teleport location that would also serve as your spawn point should you perish in combat. Staying under water until your oxygen meter is depleted would not, could not actually kill you. Instead, your vision goes black and you reappear at your subserver spawn point. These devices wouldn't work anywhere near the esplanade before or during the president's speech, however. Cunning was therefore needed. Blipping back to their spawn points with a curious liquid sound and a flash of blue light, Liz, Fresno, and the others saw the volleyball teams were just starting to warm up. It was almost showtime.

The athletes got their skimpy game suits on and started limbering themselves up. One of their avatars was customized to look like an NBA mascot, a tiger to be exact. Liz and her squad assembled and entered the tournament. From that moment on, they were another co-ed team going for the gold, and nothing else. Eric was impressed at how each member of the Seahorse Mafia had their competitive side. While Sam was the most subdued, one could tell by xyr squint that xe was calculating and was clearly having a great time. When their first match finally got underway, Maxx spiked the ball every chance he got, doing a cocky strut for the boys in the crowd.

The sun cast off its oddly discernable layers of red and purple as it approached the horizon. The squad hit the ball back and forth, played the role. When the sun finally set and the stadium lights were switched on, Liz's team knew it was almost time to rock. While they were walking off the court after throwing their last game a stray ball pelted Eric in the head. He whipped around to see the tiger mascot waving and calling with a muffled voice, *Sorry!*

Embarrassing for sure, but Eric's time to shine was coming. Nobody acknowledged him when he slipped away from the beach and headed for a skate park in the adjacent neighborhood. Eric retreated to one of the fake bathrooms, constructed entirely for entertainment rather than use, if you can believe it, and slapped the teleport button in his wrist. The next second he was standing in the back of one of the firework boats, as planned, having snuck on board to leave his respawn marker there before it left the shore.

The boatman didn't notice Eric right away. First-person gaming views had their drawbacks. Between the wind, the waves, and the beautiful, still-bright twilight, he was too distracted with appreciating the scenery and the fact that he had a very important job to do. It was true that programmers could technically manipulate matter on any subserver without needing to be in the game, but the whole point of today's event was to demonstrate Virtua's powers of simulation. Eric gulped. The trick now was dispatching the boatman without alerting any Admins.

It was too late though – or was it? The boatman looked over his shoulder, as if out of a virtual sixth sense, and Eric suddenly had to improvise. He lunged with full force and planted the kickersticker into the side of the boatman's neck. This EpiPen-like device contained a digital liquid bearing a code that would kick a player off the entire Server and all subservers for several hours, locking out their ID. The boatman grunted in protest, his consciousness fading away as he slumped down onto the floor of the boat.

In an isolated torrent of assembling pixels, President Yessica Li Lundgrasse materialized in a suite at the top of Prium's Imperial Hotel facing the distant Maraterra Sea. Greeted by an orderly line of smiling faces who were painfully eager to show her the place where she would be giving her speech, the president asked that her aides wait a moment while she took in the vesperal view. The graphics were magnificent at this distance. The president could also smell the difference in the very air of the Server compared to that of her home. She felt the carpet beneath her feet and the flesh of every hand that she shook.

"Gentlemen, ladies," the president stiffly regarded them all, "I could get used to this! I might have to stick around for a while after the speech. You guys can show me the town. I'm very excited to learn what people are doing in virtual reality today…"

The president's decisive tone tapered off not unlike that of a child who's discovered their favorite blanket has gone missing. Her gaze lingered on the suite's kitchenette, which was much too big to justify such a name. The staffers' smiles dwindled as do a campfire's last dying embers. Something was seriously wrong.

"Where is my coffee, Pete?"

One of the staffers fidgeted. Another batted him with a clipboard.

"I told you to make sure the programmers had it in here!" Yessica glared.

"They said…" Pete faltered. He'd folded the papers in his hands in half.

President Lundgrasse firmly grasped a dainty glass table and threw it with all her might into the island of the oversized kitchenette. It shattered violently, as programmed. The staffers flinched and froze.

"Get me… my goddamn… *virtual* coffee… Pete!"

"Yes sir – ma'am! Right away, ma'am!"

A presidential perimeter of secret service personnel guarded the esplanade, surrounded by thousands of players from around the world. Thousands had come, and more were on the way. Many were fans of the sport, but it was estimated that half or more were just curious bystanders on their way to do something else in the Virtua world. This presence was already being discussed on the Internet forums as ushering in a new future of the World Wide Web, and it was keeping the Monitors, NPCs, and Admins incessantly busy, something Liz had been counting on.

Liz had been putting herself in charge of planning like this for years. Organizing, strategizing, anything to stick it to The Man, really. She was a real Don't-Tread-On-Me type – no masters but over oneself. That's how she saw it. Out there in RL, there were people, whether on one side of the aisle, the other, beneath it or below it, who sought above all else to control the lives of others. Her life's mission was to burst their bubble as loudly as possible.

Liz sulked over an ongoing battle that she was still fighting inside when at last she spotted the signal she had been waiting for. The tiniest red laser flashes, three series of three short blinks, from the direction of the beach. Everything was set to go.

The tournament was fierce, and crowds were enthralled by the spectacle. They formed yahoo fanbases that altered their hair color and appearances on the fly in order to match their favorite teams' uniforms. Many got carried away in their revelry, so much that the media anchors who were standing by to shoot the president's speech were beginning to discuss cutting the crowd out of the shot. The fans were acting too obscene. Some of them were cheering and dancing so hard that they spilled out into the volleyball court during play, forcing the refs to restart the round. But President Lundgrasse put an end to that talk.

"Keep the crowds in the shot. I like it. It's raw. It's honest. It's America, damn it! Now, are we ready to go yet or what?"

In a nervous scramble, the media anchors assembled their teams, positioned their cameras, straightened their collars and ties, and waited for the president to take the podium. Lights were erected, people were hushed. The cameras started rolling. President Lundgrasse, with all her discipline and posture, asserted herself to the microphone and began with a mindful nod that bespoke an advanced sagacity, "Good evening, America."

She paused as if taken aback by the profundity of the moment.

"I speak to you now from a place that our grandparents saw

in their dreams. A future that has become the present. A dream that has become a reality." She paused again, bit both lips simultaneously as though to stifle some raw emotion, and continued. "Virtual reality has created for us a new world, a new community space where all nations can coexist and exchange ideas while remaining safely apart from each other."

Yessica looked around at the slightly jagged graphics of the press, and at her conservative supporters behind the security zone whose avatars jumped in music-fest fashion and cheered her name.

"Americans dream. It's what we are born to do. I myself have a dream – that one day we will have high enough walls, suitably impenetrable subterranean barriers, and fully weaponized sea-mine and space station perimeters to bring illegal immigration to a halt once and for all!"

After a short delay in the video relay to the edge of the audience, a great cheering was heard, underscored by a roar of people booing. Hearing that the disapproving forty-nine percent of the voting populace were present and accounted for, she leaned back from the microphone to consider her next words, tongued her teeth, then went on.

"That is the majesty, the true majesty of this invention! We can visit each other's nations, go sightseeing, eat each other's cuisine, all from the safety of our living rooms. It is a true godsend, and a true pinnacle of God's shining influence through the hands of Man." Somewhere in the crowd, Liz inaudibly groaned. "It is with great pleasure that I tell you about this—"

An unholy explosion decimated the podium and stage, obliterating all cameras and news anchors in a concussive blast and wave of fire. The only thing the audience saw was Eric's well-aimed rocket connect with the broadcasting area before a

56

wall of ejecta nullified their avatars and booted them from the Server. Gasps abounded punctuated by shrill cries.

Pandemonium ensued, the chaos of which allowed Liz and her team to easily disappear by making for the nearest portal to Barkmoor, their own private server located in Candy's house. The president and all media that had been present were instantaneously locked out of the game – Sam's coup de grace to top off the night, a system hack to complement xyr kickersticker invention, the origin of which xe would reveal only over xyr dead body.

Removing her helmet at the oval office, President Lundgrasse's eyes bugged as she looked around at the media anchors for an answer,

"*Well!* That'll be in the headlines! Where's my coffee?"

Barkmoor was the surreal product of Candy's and Sam's combined programming skills. Being a lover of fantasy novels who spent most of her offline time with her nose in a book, Candy wanted to design her private server to be the enchanted forest she'd always wanted to visit. Impossibly large trees bent and bowed this way and that, sometimes looping into knots that formed other curious shapes. The squad would be safe here. Everyone cheered Eric's smashing performance. He had already outdone his debut.

"You're one of us now!" Candy shrieked and squeezed him with her paws.

Even Maxx approved, "You really knocked it out of the park."

Sam smiled. Then Liz smiled. Eric was happy they were happy, but it was Liz's smile that went straight to his head. Now if he could only learn how to make her smile like that all the time.

For a while they all sat together on tree stumps and talked about how awesome their stunt had been. Candy acted out the explosion with her hands and body while gushing sound effects with riveting theatrics. Maxx thought to try and calm her down, but saw no harm in her celebration. She was good for times like these. She added spice to their lives and was born for celebrations. Eric expressed concern about getting into trouble, but Sam assured him to not give it a second thought.

"I mean, technically you could go viral and become famous in totally the wrong way. Nothing can really stop that, not that I think it's going to happen. But it's a videogame world. Anything goes but sex, threats, and hate crime. There are separate servers for all that."

"Uh, really?" Eric knew his country was twisted, but this twisted?

"Well, sort of. They do get their own servers as long as they don't call for violent action or overthrowing the government."

For a while the squad continued their discussion of the strange reality of chat servers made specifically for hate speech. They later made a few more toasts to their success on the esplanade. It was getting late, and soon everyone was yawning like cats. Sam and Maxx said their goodbyes, removed their helmets, and blipped out of the forest and back to their respective homes. Liz and Eric were talking about the possible effects their little stunt might have on the president's campaign when Candy abruptly yawned loud enough to interrupt their conversation,

"I'm beat. You guys stay as long as you want. Good night."

Now that they were alone, Eric felt an uncomfortable tightening in his chest accompanied by a sensation of weightlessness, almost like he was being lifted around by a little helicopter.

This was it. The pressure was on.

How could he deny that he had feelings for her? Whether these feelings were emotional or purely physical didn't matter to him at the time. Liz yawned, then was silent. She was trying to think of something to say. This was his moment. He took his shot, but when she turned her head away from his advance and emitted an uneasy sound, his high crashed like a bag of bricks.

"Listen, I like you a lot. You're, like, way more tolerable than half the guys I meet. That's it though, okay? Are we good?"

"Yeah, of course."

"Okay, good… well, I'm going to go. Have a good night."

"Good night."

Eric didn't know what else to do. He wasn't ready to go back to his life in RL yet, so he returned to the scene of the crime. Everyone had reassured him that there was nothing to worry about, so why fear it? When he got there, the multitude had dispersed. You couldn't even tell that there had been an explosion. Monitors and Admins had worked to quickly clean up the chaos. Eric tried to picture the blast radius, the blackened ground that marked the brief victory that he thought was going to finally attract a girlfriend.

Being a twenty-something-year-old virgin was… well it was confusing for Eric. He tried to forget about this, tried to remind himself how cool it was that he finally met people who wanted to be his friend. They did want to be his friend, right? A muffled voice called out with an answer, "They bailed on you already, huh?"

Eric located the source of the voice. It was Mr. Tiger Suit Mascot from the volleyball tournament. Pulling off the comically large tiger head, the man revealed his judgmental face and brownish hair. It was the stranger that Eric ran into after the treehouse ambush.

"Hey, it's you! What are you doing here?"

"Oh, I've been watching you. Don't worry, I'm not going to come on to you or anything, and I'm not a stalker. I've been watching you because I think that you have real potential, and not the kind that group of miscreants is looking for."

There was only one thing on Eric's mind: *miscreants?*

"Lester's the name." He offered a firm handshake which Eric accepted. "You do realize your only job on that last mission was to act as jailbait, right?"

This knocked Eric off balance. "What are you talking about?"

"You seem like a decent guy. I'm worried that these people aren't having the best influence on you. I might be a sneaky little spy, but I've learned things about you. You're in a lot of pain, aren't you?"

How in the fuck? Eric wasn't happy that this random stranger could just tell something like that by looking at him, unless he'd been spying on him more closely than he was letting on. Lester didn't wait for him to answer,

"Did Liz friend-zone you yet?"

That did it. Eric lost control and shoved Lester down onto the beach sand. The stranger didn't look up in fear or anger though. He was calm, collected. A series of dark thoughts passed through Eric's mind, how this wasn't real so he could beat this kid up until he'd had his fill, and there was nothing anyone could do about it. Lester rose to his feet.

"I take it that's a *Yes*."

Eric shifted his weight back onto one foot and was about to tackle the wise-ass when he started to cry. Lester showed no remorse. He went on,

"I've been where you are, Eric. I've wallowed in the darkest well of self-loathing. You know what though? I can show you how to respect yourself again – how to get women to respect you, how to make a difference in this world. What do you say?"

What the... Well now, Eric thought, *maybe there's something to this.*

"How? How can you help me?"

In the real dark of his real room, Eric lay in his real bed later that night. He was alternating between his favorite staring positions. First he stared at the ceiling, which was as blank and numb as he longed to feel, then the wall nearest to the bed, then the sole bedroom window through which he could see streetlights, branches and leaves.

Sleep would not come. Liz's face took root in his mind, that reluctantly friendly look she had given him, so very changed from the day before. *Had it really changed that much?* Eric couldn't be sure. Perhaps it was the way he saw her that changed. When he could bear it no longer, he roused from his bed and retreated to the living room couch. Television helped to numb his mind, drowning out the sound and the memories until he slipped into dreamland, where nightmares followed him.

Four

The employees at Endless Crusts Pizza Crust Factory were happy for the most part. The pay wasn't extraordinary, but the long hours inevitably resulted in decent paychecks, so they rallied. A few oddballs were estranged from the main group for one reason or another. Either they were socially awkward, uncommunicative, a stick in the mud, or bore some characteristic that killed the main group's buzz. Eric, painfully aware that he was one such oddball, spent his days chanting sentences to himself to drown out the unattainable cheer of those around him, those who reveled in each other's presence and recoiled at his.

Quit feeling sorry for yourself, he chanted inwardly. They were words he knew well, words his father had often told him. It was weird, he thought, that they had never really sunk in. No matter how many times he heard the command, he resented his loneliness, his lack of companionship, the fact that he was a virgin still – the most hilarious joke to everyone at that factory, chances were. Chances were they knew somehow. Moment to moment he fought to keep from panicking and destroying everything in his path. *Why do I think these things?* He wondered, *who am I... why do I want to tear everything apart? Senseless question begging a senseless answer.* He despaired as he watched the wretched dough. There was one thing that kept him calm at this point. One thing on which he focused his mind. Tonight, Eric would discuss theory with *him.* The theory of the involuntary celibate – the incel.

Maybe there's a message in it that will apply to me, he supposed.

Lester had instructed Eric to find the portal to the subserver called Voidwalker. After discarding another microwave dinner atop the newest pile on the kitchen floor (having neglected to take out the garbage this week), Eric entered the Virtua station, pressed the power button, and donned the helmet.

The portal to the Voidwalker subserver wasn't located on the streets of Prium, but deep down in her underbelly. Descending a series of underpass stairwells that floor by floor degraded in symmetry and lighting, Eric saw there were more cracks in the walls the further down he went. The floor got dirtier. More and more of the ceiling tiles were missing. Finally, the way down ended, leading to a tunnel of massive proportions through which two airplanes could easily pass side by side. There weren't nearly so many people here, which didn't surprise Eric much. It had taken ten minutes of stairs and hallways to get here – not exactly a riveting gaming experience.

Lester immediately spotted him from behind the curtain of his tent. Eric walked through the cavernous, arch-roofed space and heard Lester's bassoon of a voice muttering about something. Eric drew closer. As he'd been told, he could tell which among the smattering of drab, patched-up tents was Lester's by the black flag that was suspended from a pole outside. With no wind to blow it, the flag appeared dormant, asleep.

"You got a narrow jaw, kid," Lester jeered. "You know what that means? It only has everything to do with your misfortune."

Displeased to be so soon reminded of his predicament, Eric scowled, but held on. He had a feeling that there was something to be gained from this Lester character, who sat on a simple cot and swiped his right index finger through the air in varying patterns. In his mind, Lester could have been doing anything – reading, chatting, searching for something. Finally he made eye contact with Eric as he sat down in the cot across from him.

"Welcome."

Eric nodded in reply, thoroughly confused. Here they were in the crowning achievement of videogaming technology, and this man was sitting on a cot in a tent at the bottom of nowhere. Why?

Eric asked, "Where are we? What are all of you doing down here?"

Lester's face was blank as he gathered a simple tea kettle and poured himself a cup. Offering some to Eric but receiving a headshake in turn, Lester sipped and sighed, "Do you suppose we could really be anywhere else?"

This felt like a trick question, but Eric tried his best. "Of course we could be. We could have met in Prium, or on a real subserver, or maybe in RL even. I mean, what is this place? What's the point of coming down here at all?"

"You ask all the wrong questions, squirt." Lester dismissively broke eye contact to focus on his tea. Eric didn't appreciate the little pet name. "What you ought to ask is: 'Now that I'm here, what am I going to do next?' That's all that matters, don't you think? What we do from here."

Eric felt a contrarian nerve twitch, but he accepted this. It was all that really mattered to him in that moment, he could agree. Ending his sorrow. Ending his loneliness. Ending the moments when he thinks he has friends but then they turn out to be phonies.

"Your jaw, let's talk about it." Lester straightened himself up. He held a monk-like posture with a demeanor that was the shape of wisdom. "It's like this place, isn't it? What sense would it be to ask, 'Why do I have this jaw?', beyond scientific study, when nothing can change the fact that you're here now. You have the jaw you were born with."

Eric thought Lester's attitude was getting old fast. It was depressing, and what was it meant to teach him? He would entertain it only a little longer, he decided, and said, "But we're in the Virtua world. We can look however we want to look. You can just choose to have a bigger jaw here."

"Precisely. And yet you look just that same as you did in RL. Why is that?" Lester leaned into his accusatory question.

Eric had no ready answer for this, and the more he thought about it, the more it disturbed him. Lester chuckled, which made Eric even angrier.

"Glad you think this is so funny."

"See? There you go, doing it again."

"Doing what?" Violent thoughts began to germinate inside Eric.

"Saying what people expect you to say. Embracing destiny instead of shaping it. Fact is you could have chosen to look like The Hulk, Superman, or Dwayne 'The Rock' Johnson, but you picked what nature gave you. Let me ask you something, are you a virgin?"

Eric exploded onto his feet and stormed out of the tent. *Enlightened wiseman my ass.* Visions of past rejections swirled in his head, speckled with the memory of Liz's reluctant smile. *Monster. Loser.* He had no reason to see himself as anything else. And what did his fucking jaw have to do with it? In one last irritatingly well-perceived observation, Lester called after him, asking, "Don't you want to know what your jaw has to do with it?"

65

Eric slowed his pace and faltered to an eventual stop. His fists balled up. What was he doing here? He was supposed to be playing videogames. That's what this helmet thing was for, not talking to assholes who made him hate himself. *Didn't you already hate yourself though?* He couldn't help but ask. Turning around, he saw Lester was the calm opposite to his own irritation.

"What? What does it have to do with anything?"

Lester cast a long gaze down the massive tunnel, took a deep breath, "Walk with me."

There are psychopomps and other guides in America and across the globe whose messages resonate with millions yet conflict with the messages of others. Accusations of false teachers and prophets abound. To Lester, it was necessary to acknowledge that the majority of prevailing teachers, those whose lessons influenced the manners of society at large, were fundamentally flawed in their thinking.

"A person's life is not a videogame," he said while they walked. "You can't just customize your character and look however you want. You could get transgender surgery, you could get plastic surgery, and you could even try some really weird, experimental stuff using silicone, but there are parts to your human form that you cannot escape."

Lester wasn't blaming or making fun of Eric for choosing his own appearance – he was admiring it.

"A person cannot escape himself, so accepting his appearance is the noblest path, one that you, Eric, admirably wear on your sleeve as far as I can tell."

Advancing in a professor's march, Lester, arms behind his back, regarded Eric's hurt look of gratitude briefly, then went on,

"As for your jaw, the running theory among the incels is

called *mandibular determinism*, which states that inceldom, or the state of being an incel, has a very concrete cause, and is in fact predictably and inextricably linked to a male's appearance. This predetermined manifestation of one's DNA is the tip of the philosophical iceberg that we call *the blackpill way.*

"*Redpill* thinkers, on the other hand, believe self-improvement is the way out of inceldom, that they can work on themselves in some way or another to escape their fate. There are undeniable ways that this is true, surgeries and what have you, but just think – you can't escape the fact that you must eat food. You must breathe the air, ache when in pain. And when that *foid* Liz turned you down cold, how did it make you feel?"

The two walked along the outer edge of the grand tunnel. Others were walking too, though far separated from each other, alone. It was yet another sorely confusing sight to see in Virtua, Eric thought. The murky scene was that of a dank brutalism locked away in a vast cellar. The uninterrupted stretches of concrete wall were broken only by the odd crack or water stain, and the people were so morose it seemed they themselves might soon be coated in grime.

"It hurt. It felt like my guts were being torn out." Eric fought back tears, too proud to hurt so openly in front of Lester. "Why does it have to hurt so much?"

"It's because you are a man. You aren't a sexual deviant either – you want what nature makes you to want, and that's the roastie."

"...the roastie?"

"Pussy, vag, pun tang."

"Oh..."

"The answer lies all around us, friend. Think about it. When two bucks want a doe, what do they do?"

"…they fight."

"Damn right they do, and they eff each other up if they can. Might even kill each other. Humans do it too, all the time. Don't believe me? Just ask anyone that works in law enforcement."

Eric didn't like where this was going as they plodded on through the murk. He could entertain notions of predestination, but this blackpill way…

Well, he supposed, *there are those birds and frogs and all sorts of other animals that choose mates based on how well they can do something. Anatomy could have something to do with success in nature.* He shook his head to rid himself of that thought. People weren't animals. That was an age-old understanding. There was something that set us apart from our critter cousins. Were there exceptions to this?

He wasn't sure, and didn't want to think about it either, but Lester pressed him, "Let's put the theory to the test. What do you say? We have a unique opportunity here, don't we?"

Lester ushered Eric into another tent which on the outside looked the same as his own, but inside there was a steady ring of light interwoven with flowing streams of sparks that cracked and snapped with energy. The wispy ring gave off an intense glow.

"No need to log out and start a new character. Step into the ring, and we'll make your adjustments."

Hesitant at first, Eric did as he was asked. Stepping into the light suddenly cut off all stimulation from the Virtua world. He could neither hear any sound nor smell the air. After a span of eerie quiet he at last began to hear static. White noise. Distant but building, like an approaching wave about to break on a shoreline. Standing outside the ring and still linked to the Virtua server, Lester smiled fiercely as he pulled at invisible dials and pressed invisible buttons.

Eric's body had the sensation of being turned into playdough as he stretched out taller. His jaw widened, his wrists became girthy. This made him feel powerful, just like Lester said it would. Lester spoke to Eric while making the adjustments to his avatar. He elaborated on how there were theories about the wrist as well as the jaw. Apparently, size matters. He was right. Eric could feel the power. He had become superior. Improved. But would it make any difference if he acted awkward and lame?

"It's time for a test drive," Lester declared. He then stepped into the ring of light to join Eric, coming so close as to make him uncomfortable. "To the club!" He waved his wrist, and the two of them disappeared.

Five

"Hey! Do you guys want to know what one of the hardest things about being a ferret is?"

Maxx, who was unhappy that Candy had thoughtlessly posted a selfie with his artwork in the background, snapped back, "You are what you eat, so… is it that you're a rat? A stinking, lying rat?"

Sam slugged Maxx in his gargantuan arm to little effect. He only frowned at her. It was the gesture, not Sam's knuckles, that hurt.

"What? She spoiled the surprise! Do you know how long it took me to make that sculpture? She promised she wouldn't. It's my masterpiece. My *masterpiece*, you got that? Even if it's only temporary."

Candy squirreled around the erect penis statue, apologizing in an otherwise idle manner while she admired and photographed every bulging vein, every curve and dip. One would have thought the whole scene to be phallic worship were it not for what Liz did next.

Liz didn't hate men. Maxx was one of her best friends, and he was a man. No, whenever she asked to have a penis sculpture erected and then burned it down, whether in VR or in RL, it was about freedom. Freedom from control. Freedom from being forced to bow to the phallus or worship the phallus. Freedom from getting screwed out of her Goddess-given right to life and a voice. She didn't blame Candy for ruining the surprise once she had led Liz to the statue's location in front of Chrome Tigers' former lair, which the squad had decided to occupy and defend as a lasting insult to their nemeses.

"It's hard because, when you're a ferret, you can't – stop – moving – *what* is *that*, Liz?" Candy exploded with more excitement than usual. She zipped around and all over the statue until stopping finally at the tip-top. There was a weapon in Liz's hands that none of them recognized. The best way to describe it was an AK made out of pure crystal.

"I found this baby in the basement. You better believe it'll come in handy."

Liz slowly took aim. Feeling vulnerable at the look of her hungry stare, Candy scurried off the statue. By the time she hit the ground, Liz had fired a single explosive round that decimated the head of the penis, shattering it into thousands of pixelated fragments. The whole squad cheered.

Eric was neck-deep in results. There was no denying it – the jaw and wrist amplifications had done the trick. A mature-only dance club subserver call Hop-In permitted all legally programmable forms of contact. This meant that he could feel a woman's touch as if she were a real woman when she pressed up against him, licked his neck and ears, or grabbed his ass on the dance floor. Yet privacy laws meant no one could rightly say what anyone else's sex was in RL. What he couldn't feel, what none of them could feel, were their loins. The loins had been disabled in accordance with specific legislation. This did not entirely render mature-only subservers as useless, however. The rest of people's bodies still experienced the surface-level hormone spikes that occurred in all the other sensual experiences that were possible without involving the genitals.

At first the experience was everything Lester promised it would be, everything Eric imagined it would be. A veil had been lifted, a burden released, like a trained hawk set to flight. This relief however did not last. A spooked feeling crept into his head when he looked into the eyes of his fellow clubgoers the closer they danced. He wasn't sure whether they were actually women, couldn't decide whether being able to tell mattered, and taunting him was the ultimate reality that none of it was real, that he still had to be regular elf-jawed Eric with the weak, limp wrists when he went back to work the next day, where everyone would laugh at him like they always did.

Eric slackened his grip on the ladies that surrounded him and eventually pulled away from them entirely. He took a good look at all the dancers around the club. Lester appeared at his side.

"You're thinking of backing out, aren't you?"

"I'll get kicked for a day. It's not that bad."

"That's right. It's nothing. It's just a first step."

A first step, Eric chanted in his head. It was a game. The flirting, the touching, the fake people telling real lies. *Fine then,* he decided. *A first step.*

Not wasting another second, Eric pushed the next woman to cross his path off the balcony that overlooked the swanky nightclub. The shrill sound of terror filled the air, and her scream brought most of the club to a momentary standstill. It was easy to forget that it was only VR. Noticing that Lester had disappeared, Eric unleashed his fury for what he intended to be a final time by grabbing the nearest woman or supposed woman by the hair and slinging her off the balcony as well. Drunk with rage, he forced himself onto the next one to cross his path, a strong, willful young woman who head butted him to little effect. He wrestled her to the ground.

I'm not a monster. This isn't real. It's a videogame. It's harmless, he told himself as the woman struggled and shrieked beneath him. She was a real person though, one with real feelings who really felt him on top of her, who watched him menacingly stare down at her. She blipped into nothing, gone without a trace. She must have removed her Virtua helmet. Forever slipped through his fingers. No chance to abuse, no chance to ask forgiveness. He asked himself, *Do I even want forgiveness?*

Eric stood on the balcony of his apartment drinking a cola. Not only had he been suspended for a minimum of one month, but the Virtua brand threatened legal action if they ever heard about anything like this ever again, especially if it involved him. They said no one behaved as poorly as he had in the scant weeks since the Server had gone live, but it was still a new realm. Indeed, Eric's story would prove to be one in a long line of cases.

Eric felt a million times worse than he ever had. He didn't stop torturing himself for a single second after he got booted off the Server and his Virtua helm went dark. The images of what he had done flashed through his mind. He couldn't escape them. Just as before, his Self was the problem, only now it begged the question – had it been worth it? Was there some truth to Lester's message which resonated so deeply with Eric that it expelled all the pent-up frustration he'd buried inside himself over the years? He considered all these things until he noticed someone walking far below the balcony. It was an odd time for someone to be out – four a.m. Stranger still was the buzz that sounded at his apartment door. Someone wanted to be let in.

He had seen enough scary movies. Eric wasn't going to simply let the stranger come inside without any information, whoever they were. His heartbeat galloped in the elevator which suddenly gave off the vibe of a potential death trap. *In the movies, people are always getting killed in elevators.* What might be waiting when the doors opened? *No,* he reminded himself, *the security door is a good distance from the elevator hall, and the glass walls are unbreakable.* Remembering this didn't help much. Eric imagined watching the elevator doors peel open to reveal the face of a man, a man who, just as Eric himself had behaved in the club, was about to lose control. The doors rolled open, revealing no sinister snarl. Only the darkened all-white elevator hall, empty but for its office décor of neutral landscape paintings and potted ferns.

Coming out of the hall and turning the corner, Eric looked down the empty lobby to see Lester waiting there at the door. He held a piece of paper against the glass with the hashtag *#Statusmaxx* thickly scrawled in pencil.

"Get a load of this fucking *pathetic* dude," Liz sneered.

Her squad gathered 'round. They needed a break from mountain climbing on a scale model of the Sierra Nevada. It was a brilliant model, and very well done, Sam thought. The artificial sun baked their skin to the point they felt sunblock would be necessary, but of course ignored this impulse without concern.

Liz had drawn a floating chat window which she was using to scroll through Virtua's social network. Some incel creepazoid was preaching the control of women's bodies over the public feed, and she wasn't about to let that slide. Her friends always found this side of her entertaining. Watching her rip into someone online was like watching a champion boxer enter the ring.

T. K. O.

"*The violence of men can be attributed directly to the sexuality of women,* I mean have you ever heard such a pile of fecal verbiage?" Liz shook her head. "More like, *you have to have sex with me or I'll kill you.* Oh ho, this *Runsdeep99* guy is going to regret spewing his bullshit."

Liz drilled away at her keyboard before resolving at last to record a video rant to post in the comments in place of a multi-part essay. Gesturing with the execution of a pro influencer, she called Runsdeep99 out as having been born in the wrong century, just like every other bigoted mansplainer who tried to tell women that all the world's ills were their doing. She laced into him vehemently, not pulling a punch. Runsdeep99 suggested that if she had ever turned someone down in her life, she would understand.

Wow so u fr think I've never turned down a guy b4 otherwise I'd understand? Ya-a-a I just turned a dude down the other day. Guy thought there was something when there wasn't. And yeah he got all glum but I'm not trying to have anybody tell me that's a sign that I g2 bang him or else. All you incel creeps need to seriously fuck off and stay off the public chat boards.

Runsdeep99 apologized, acted offended at the suggestion that he should keep his idea to himself, then asked if the guy she dumped would appreciate what she's saying.

The two of you can commit yourselves to a mental institution because there's no talking to crazy. #Sorrynotsorry

"Who's the guy you're talking about?" Candy asked. Liz hadn't told her friends about Eric's recent attempted kiss.

"Nobody, I just felt like bringing the pain to this jerk."

"Nice. You ready to go yet?"

"Yeah, let's send it." Liz strapped on her snowboard and inched herself to the edge of the slope with her friends. Counting to three, they dropped all at once and carved into the powdery landscape, pulled down by the merciless gravity.

Lester waited patiently while Eric cried his eyes out. This wasn't his first grooming, but Eric's sobs were still a haunting sound. Lester had watched soul after soul bawl the night away over some woman on whom their unrequited love had been tragically wasted. It made him sick. *This has to end,* Lester thought angrily to himself. *All of it.*

"What are you doing?" Lester asked, finally losing his patience.

Eric sniffled and whined, answered hesitantly, "I'm upset, okay?"

"You're crying. You can't help it though, can you? Of course you can't help it. You're a man. You have a need to pass on your genes. It's your only practical purpose for existing, the only reason that you're alive. It runs deep down into your DNA. Feelings, feminine indecision – these things are not you, but unnatural nails driven through you to hold you down, to keep you from becoming the man you are. Is it the truth that hurts, or are you just unwilling to let her go?"

"What does that matter?"

Lester didn't answer, and Eric went back to weeping. It was a process, as Lester knew well. You had to plant a seed, make them ask the question, then let it fester. Having asked the question, their mind won't cease to run until the answer is found. Their sorrow won't let them stop. That was his understanding. Give that man time, and he will get to his feet, and eventually he'll be willing to take action. *If you've got the right man,* Lester mused, *he'll take just about any action that dulls the pain.*

Eric bellowed, "How did you find me?" Eric hadn't thought to ask this earlier. When he let Lester inside, instead of saying anything, Lester showed Eric his tablet and his recent conversation with Liz on the chat board. Eric didn't think anything of it at first. He even figured that Lester had it coming. Then he saw how Lester got her to mention Eric's rejection.

"I'm a hacker – a good one."

"And what does Statusmaxx mean?" Eric wiped his eyes.

"We say X-maxx, Y-maxx to stress the extremely high advantages of chads and the sex that they're thus afforded. Looksmaxx, statusmaxx, these mean you have superior looks, superior wealth.

"*We? Chads?*" Eric questioned.

"You must know who I represent by now. You saw what Liz said. As for chads, chads are people who succeed at sex. They are the opposite of incels."

Eric was torn. Liz had hurt him, and in his misery, it felt natural to protest the state of society, to blame society for what ailed him. But Lester was advocating for the complete control of woman's bodies, down to their choice (or not) of sexual partner. He cringed to think what other rules Lester might find necessary.

"Liz hurt me, but I don't want to hurt her back."

"The plan was never to attack those voids, Eric. You were supposed to neg them, tell them off and assert yourself, but instead you acted like a child. That is not what I'm trying to show you."

What then? Lester didn't answer the questioning face that Eric wore. He simply went on with his speech, "You can't change a woman, Eric, just like you can't change a man. We want what we want, and as soon as the world figures that out, the sooner we'll get respect and stop being the butt of every joke for not convincing some roastie to sit on our laps."

"Black pill or red pill…" Eric noted out loud. Lester nodded.

Eric questioned everything about himself, who he was, what

his goals were, what he wanted out of life, and Lester could see it in him. Deep inside, Lester was cackling and rubbing his hands together. He'd done it. The seed had sprouted. Its roots were digging into Eric's mind. Now, to water it.

"Not everyone can handle it. Some want to fight the system, some want to just accept it and learn to live without the voids. Which one are you?"

Eric didn't know what he wanted, who he was, or what his intentions for the future were. Ultimately there were two glaring facts he couldn't deny. First, Liz was the spoonful of neutron star that broke the camel in half and sank it down into the center of the Earth. Second, Lester and his ideas were going to turn heads. Most people would probably hate him because most people didn't have a hard time having sex at some point in their lives, or even on a regular basis. Eric's breath shook the more he realized it all boiled down to sex somehow. Or was Lester simply a master propagandist? Eric wrestled with himself inside. He had to do something, he knew that much.

"It's over. It never even began. There is no path. There never was. All that we do now and tomorrow must reflect our embracing of that fact," Lester declared.

It felt like being an astronaut lost in space, facing the question of what actions he would be willing to take in order to escape the pain. Eric tried to find a thought of his own. It was there somewhere. The right thing to do. The choice he had to make. No one else could make it for him. In dramatic, sweeping fashion, Lester threw open a rolled up blueprint on Eric's dining room table.

"Our only task is to spread the message."

Six

It took six hours to drive all the way to the VirtuaHelm™ headquarters in Santa Clara. Lester's 2038 Netopyr was an average ride, but it hugged the asphalt beneath the black night. Lester kept his eyes glued to his laptop the whole time while Eric drove, having used his once-per-week manual override excuse as permitted by law. Driving around the perimeter to take in the central building, Eric saw a glass-covered structure nearly wide as it was tall, somewhere between a box and a pyramid. He had read once that there was space for ten helicopters to land on the roof.

Pulling over on the side of a quiet, immaculately clean city street at Lester's request, Eric's heart started to race. Lester's grand scheme was about to unfold, and Eric wasn't seeing any reason to resist it. What direction did he have in his own life, after all? Lester had a plan, a philosophy, a list of wrongs to right, all of which gave Eric a new purpose. It made him think he could make a difference too, even if it didn't mean changing his own fate. Lester pored through dozens of pages of literature, not explaining any of it to Eric, who suddenly recalled Lester's odd word that he used in place of *girls* or *women*.

"Why do you call them *voids*, Lester?"

Lester's eyes trailed off from the screen and gradually met Eric's.

"Femoids, or foids. Chicks. Since we can't have them, to us they are nothing, so 'void' is a nice adaptation of 'foid', don't you think?"

Not a person – a person-like creature, Eric thought. His gut felt uneasy.

Feelings aren't imaginary. Eric's pain was real. His confusion and his frustration with the world were just as real as his decision to join Lester on his crusade, as was the feeling in his stomach.

"That's okay. You don't have to answer. It never feels right at first. You'll come to understand it eventually. The black pill only refers to our dilemma – sex. We are still men. We still have hands and emotions and willpower. We can shape things to better suit our cause, and it's high time I show you how."

Lester reached back into the car, flipped a switch on a boxy amalgamation of cords and electrical devices, and pulled a pair of headsets into the front cabin. Wires neatly arranged and woven into sturdy ropes stemmed from the backs of the headsets and connected to the device array in the back seat. Pulling one over his own head, Lester nodded at Eric to do the same.

The place they appeared next could be described as standing in an elevator with mirrors on the walls. All around them, versions of themselves stretched forever into the distance, mirror images in every way. They were all doing a kind of bizarre dance. Eric wondered, *is that the 90s baby Internet dance?* Then one of them started to do something very strange. No, two of them. One of Lester and one of Eric.

As Eric watched, the two deviant copies stopped mimicking all the random movements that were being performed by the others in perfect unison and stepped away from the line of reflections like football players leaving the field. Before Eric could ask Lester what was going on, the conforming duplicates began collapsing backwards onto each other in a cascade effect that rushed from a crawl to a zipping speed, fusing Eric and Lester together with all the copies. Then everything went white.

Sam was the only one in the squad who couldn't relate to the whole sexual tension thing in the slightest. Being asexual, the whole conflict was a mystery to xem, and that especially went for the boys-versus-girls duality, Mars versus Venus, fiery explosions and belching contests versus manicures and shopping – the strict, old-school prescriptivist duality that xe and xyr squad always made fun of, ancient gender culture and roles that were fading fast with time, lingering in pockets whom Liz referred to unkindly as *cavemen*.

Hetero Liz had her fair share of drama to share with the group, and stories of Candy's old lesbian escapades were the stuff of legend. As for Maxx, boy trouble had never really been a problem for him. He just didn't do drama, so he'd drop a dude in a heartbeat, no questions asked. Cut-off King, that was Maxx. This would inspire Liz on occasion to delete her own toxic relationship from her life. Not today, however. Today she was lamenting how fragile guys could be, still feeling disappointed in her soured friendship with *Errigo*.

"I just hate that whenever I start to have a good relationship with a guy he tries to get in my pants. So I respond to a guy's intentions sometimes?" She shrugged with palms to the air, then, eyes rolling, she gagged dismissively and waved the gesture away. "I just wish it wasn't all so predictable. It would have been sweet to add another member to our crew. Maybe there's just no hope for cisgender hetero bros."

Candy cried in disbelief, "Holy crap! Somebody is hacking into the Server!"

Everyone froze, looked at Candy, saw her eyes staring into space,

81

clearly glued to the public news feed, then they opened up their own screens and read the headlines:

ROGUE HACKERS INFILTRATE VIRTUA SERVER ARCHITECTURE.
Security Personnel Consider Shutting Down Server, Virus May Remain Active
WANT TO SEE our security staff in action? Tap here.

The fun house of mirror reflections was replaced by an infinite series of lime green grids that looked like fractals of pavilion rafters. In the deep background of things there was nothing. A true void. Empty blackness an immeasurable distance away. Lester and Eric clung to the grid like kids on a jungle gym of galactic magnitude. Eric watched as bright lights appeared in the distance beyond the edges of the grid, watched them glide along the perfectly square corridors that ran in six directions. The lights grew brighter, revealing themselves to be beings of light with radiant power arcing at their fingertips. Eric urged Lester on. "What now? Do something!"

"I am…" Lester replied, his eyes focused on his invisible screen. Timing was everything now. Mentally they were inside this visual representation of the computer matrix, but physically they were still in the parking lot across from Virtua headquarters, meaning their illicit access to the Server now had the potential to do some serious damage.

If Lester could break past a final layer of security, he could download a chunk of game interaction history. Eric hadn't understood why this mattered, so Lester explained it during the drive. Identities are protected through the Server. Nobody other than you and the company can prove that you are who you say

82

you are. Exposing the private activities of certain individuals could lend the cause enough fuel and leverage to reach targets of successively higher relevance. It was no use bothering to change the behavior of foids, Lester had argued, but that didn't mean there wasn't any work to be done. Eric hated himself for entertaining what Lester was suggesting, yet here they were.

"Hurry!"

"Shh!"

The beings of light were completely visible now and took up nearly half of the space in the corridors. Brutish creatures, their faces were solemn and unchanging, with eyes of pure, blinding brilliance. Their limbs and shoulders all seemed bound as if fused together, making them look like massive chess pieces. Peering hard, Eric saw however that their arms were slowly opening, forming an interconnected flow of particles.

Lester ordered, "Let go!"

"What?"

Lester said no more. He let himself fall backwards and plummeted rapidly toward the being that approached from below. Trusting the moment, Eric dove after him headfirst. The light-man rushed up to destroy them when suddenly a section of grid closed up around Eric and Lester, forming an impenetrable barrier through which the luminous entity could not pass. These enforcer beings, the Admins, barked and raged outside this artificial shell, their limitless energy rendered useless against the power of the grid itself.

Green wires wrapped around Eric and Lester, making the growing dozens of security Admins less visible with every passing moment. Then came the noise. A high-treble popping sound like little metal nubs striking a metallic surface in rapid succession, mixed with the grating yawn of an old rusty door. It grew louder until the space beyond the new section was invisible, the blackness gone. Only a glowing green sphere some ten feet wide remained with Eric and Lester floating inside.

"They've made it to the mainframe!" Candy was ecstatic and loving this latest bit of drama, and wasn't beyond rooting for the hackers until the names of the identified individuals were displayed in the feed.

Liz read the words posted in an official Virtua staff article, "Perpetrators identified as rogue avatars of illicit production..." she gazed intently at photos taken of the avatars. She couldn't have possibly known that Eric was beneath one of the shoddy custom skins. She read further and learned that the Server would not be shut down yet, the explanation being that it was still possible for the implanted virus to remain active despite any shutdown. Virtua officials were urging players to exercise caution and to consider logging off until the situation was neutralized. Then Liz read another headline.

"You son of a bitch."

Runsdeep99 was the name of one of the hackers. The other was Runsdeep1. Whoever they were, their hacking achievement was already being hailed as fiendishly impressive, since Virtua had promised months ago that hacking would be impossible on their Server. The friends spent a short time reading more on the situation before retreating to Barkmoor, where they continued to monitor the news feeds.

Media outlets were speculating incessantly on what repercussions the hackers might face, as some believed their arrest to be inevitable. Some organizations guessed that Virtua would not be able to prosecute the infiltrators due to personal protections stipulated in their user agreement. Then the victims started coming forward.

One channel aired a piece, then another featuring a different victim. It was swiftly understood that this wasn't the first time the name *Runsdeep* had made headline news. A few years prior there had been a spate of hacker attacks against LGBTQIA+ rally organizers in the state of California. Liz cussed at the realization that she hadn't just spoken with any old incel, she had spoken with The Incel, if it was indeed just one man. The sudden appearance of a second Runsdeep title seemed to indicate a following, though perhaps it had been a group all along.

The inside of the green glowing sphere expanded in a slow, rhythmic pulse. A transparent glass-like bridge appeared beneath Eric and Lester which allowed them to put their feet down. Eric looked down at the fingers and palms that were not his. He had finally stepped out of his skin, but it was for a much different purpose than he had originally imagined.

"We're safe in here for now," Lester said. He sat cross legged on the clear bridge and swiped his fingers around in the air. Eric quickly grew tired of waiting, but he knew it wouldn't be much longer before it would all be over.

Lester noticed something was off. The previous apprehension was gone from Eric. He could feel it in the air. He halted his calculations for a moment and regarded his recruit, "Once I've tapped into the gameplay storage files, we'll be able to download, log out, and hit the road before they even know what hit them."

Eric remained silent and didn't look at him. Lester didn't like it. Something was definitely off. Lester went back to swiping and searching, but continued to speak, "You're having second thoughts, aren't you?"

Eric said nothing.

"We're in too deep. If you back out now, we'll set the cause back by months, if not years. I need your help restoring the files once we're on the road again in RL."

Then Lester saw it. There in the code, the encroaching volley of commands that layer by layer were unlocking his protective sphere. Somehow, someone on the outside was tapping into his pirate broadcasting hardware. It could mean only one thing: someone had found them. Someone had found their bodies.

This time, when Lester looked at Eric, he saw not the face of a reluctant recruit who was getting cold feet, but the face of a traitor.

"It was you."

Eric made eye contact a final time before reaching toward the back of his head, but Lester gestured with one hand to override his log-out, freezing Eric where he stood. Torn between worlds, Eric could feel the back of his head, yet those same fingers felt instead the back of his VR helmet. He pulled, he yanked. He was sure he was about to tear his own head off trying to remove the helmet. Lester tried to look into Eric's eyes, but he tore away, so instead he tackled him down onto the increasingly narrow floor. Strands of green wire snapped and flew loose of the sphere, revealing the sparks and blackness of the architectural construct beyond. Eric's fingertips melted into his skull and his hair as he tore at the back of his head. Lester, eyes wide, face twisted, voice quaking with rage, grasped Eric's throat, "I know where you live. You'll never be safe. Don't bother sleep—"

At last the helmet ripped free, having been removed by a police officer who opened the driver-side door and helped Eric out of the car. The rush of wet, cold night air was a shock to Eric's tech-stimmed mind. As the police escorted him away, he looked back to see Lester lying in the passenger-side seat, his mouth ajar, tears running down his cheeks.

Seven

"Are you going to answer the question or do you want us to take you back to your cell?"

"I'm not saying anything without a lawyer."

Santa Clara Police were at something of a loss on what to do with Lester. It had been hours since his arrest, and still nobody from Virtua had come into the station to initiate proceedings. They may have just wanted to let their captured hacker stew in jail for the weekend before cracking him on Monday. Officers had been put on high alert the second that the company learned from Eric's call that they were about to be hacked, later discovering Lester's car and the two unresponsive individuals inside. As for Lester's homemade VirtuaHelm^{TM}, he would only admit that his design was superior in that it did not require a sophisticated track system to contain the player's movements. All movements were contained within the mind, meaning that his tethering system, though physical rather than wireless, was much more sophisticated than the company's existing technology. How he had achieved this he would not say, nor anything else on the topic. Not without a lawyer. Problem was that the officers couldn't bring in a lawyer yet since they needed to await the company's instructions before the prosecution could get to work. Finally, they left him alone in a cell with nothing but four walls, a bed, a pillow and a shitter. Virtua would have twenty-four hours to make up their minds.

The hours passed. Lester didn't keep track. He didn't wonder how long he had left, nor did he wonder whether he was in any trouble. No, revenge was his focus now. Revenge for Eric's betrayal. Their mission was supposed to have been the snowball that would grow into an avalanche for the blackpill cause. Ruining people's lives sounded cruel. Lester knew that. What he didn't appreciate was anyone misunderstanding or reducing the value of his work, of his philosophy, to that of a bitter rage, because to Lester it was much more than that.

This is about putting women in their place, he thought, *and ending the root of all evil that has necessitated the blackpill way.* Eric was going to pay dearly, but how? *Shall I focus on ruining his life? Exposing his activities with me?* It wouldn't be new territory. Lester had done it before, and he would do it again. Thoughts began to creep in of his hatred for women, for himself, for people like Eric who should have been his friend but failed him like all the rest in the end.

Time ceased to exist, and in its place was the distorted wrath in every breath that Lester took, the seething hate inside his every particle.

World-destroyer.

It could have been two or ten hours later when the cell door finally opened. Lester's consciousness had been wavering in and out with the roiling of his madness. Officers ordered him to get up, then escorted him to an interrogation room. Lester could tell it was the middle of the night by the empty blackness beyond the meager hallway windows. Seated at the table of the interrogation room was a man in a suit. *This is it,* Lester assumed. *Time to face the music.*

"Hello," the man offered a hand to Lester. After brief hesitation, Lester shook the hand and took his seat. The Suit, who had all the body language of your run-of-the-mill bigwig corporate type, nodded for the police officers to leave them alone in the room. Lester was impressed. Before speaking further, the man took a long swig of iceless water that held no sparkle beneath the semi-dimmed lights.

"That was really impressive what you pulled off today. We've had our fair share of hacking attempts, but nothing like what you achieved. And this," with a delicate touch, The Suit removed from a manila folder photographs of Lester's homemade VR system and spread them out on the desk, "well this is my new favorite thing in the world."

The man examined the photographs for what must have been the dozenth time. "How did you do it? I mean really, *how* did you do it? Because I have access to the best of the best. I'm talking high-level military contract stuff. How did you manage to create something like this? I want a straight answer."

Lester's face relaxed. He raised his brow as though surprised.

"I'm self-taught. That is all you need to know."

"Oh that's good, yes that's very good," The Suit chuckled as he gathered the photos and slid the manila folder aside. He folded his hands, teetering on the cusp of some number of emotions, and looked straight into Lester's eyes. Lester looked back, unbothered by the direct attitude or the irritated underlayer that screamed *I'm-going-to-break-you*. Lester recognized another layer just above it, one that admired Lester, one that wanted to understand him.

"Although," Lester began, "perhaps we can arrange some sort of exchange?" He kept his face plain, showed no emotion.

"What could I possibly give you? Money?"

"No. I want something that is much more useful to me than money."

"What is it, then?"

Lester stood up slowly from his seat. This made The Suit a little nervous, causing him to stir with concern, but Lester walked to one of the room's corners, lowered his head, and spoke softly, "I'll give you my designs. All of them. Of course you could try to back-engineer the helmet, but you'll have to figure out the programming language that I invented first. Good luck with that. Let me save you the time. Let me *give* you my designs, but in return I ask only one thing of you." His smile, hidden in the corner, was devious.

The Suit leaned in, curious, eager.

Although reuniting with Liz and the squad was easier than Eric or rather *Errigo* expected, he was still a virgin, as well as delicate by nature, so the whole unrequited affection thing was awkward. Eric decided he would have to be selective with his focuses. Hounding for Liz's attention would obviously be counterproductive. If she had any inward thoughts about him, it was entirely up to her whether to share it, and trying to keep alive any incessant conversation would only prove annoying.

There was also the fact that he'd been temporarily recruited by a crazed incel hacker who was hellbent on curbing women's rights and spreading his misogynist dogma. None of the others knew Lester like he did, so they didn't expect they'd ever be hearing any more news about the man. No, the squad had racing on their minds.

The crew of friends accepted Eric's presence readily without question, while Maxx of course limited his friendliness to the odd smirk. Everyone was in agreement on one thing: it was time to get back to videogames – the real reason for being on the Server.

"I say we hit Isonia. Get away from the weapons and

mayhem for a while. Strictly racing," Maxx suggested as the crew reclined at the Terrazza chat club, a bright complex of interconnecting rooms and buildings done in both pastel and vivid neon colors not unlike a coral reef.

"Just kill me now. It'll be quicker than being bored to death," Candy complained. Her long, snow-white coat bristled as she stretched and yawned on a couch. The ferret sank deeper into the cushions. Liz had been panning through screens in her invisible window that listed and detailed the various games available to play. Racing had been suggested, but which racing game to choose?

"Come on, haven't you had enough of all the craziness? Let's bring things back down to Earth for a while. I'm not saying we play NASCAR but let's get behind the wheel of a muscle car or something, are you with me?" Maxx's voice was deep and full of juice. His enthusiasm was contagious.

Atypical for xyr usual start to a night of gaming, Sam joined in, "I'm with Maxx. Come on, people! What do you say?"

Candy writhed a bit more and emitted some unintelligible sounds akin to unhappy grunts or moans. Liz and Eric exchanged a humored glance and laughed. Maxx was already looking up the location of the portal.

"This way!"

Ken Faraday wasn't an involuntary celibate. He would have been better described as a *chad*, seeing as how many saw him as an alpha and a pickup artist. After listening to Lester proselytize his philosophy on why women should be kept at home and traded as assets, however, Ken began to have a vision of a different kind of future. Their meeting at the police department wouldn't have given them enough time to go over everything Lester had to say, so he invited Ken to walk with him down in the caverns below Prium. There, he would explain his ideas in detail, and this would be the only condition to gaining access to Lester's designs.

Ken's father had warned him, just as Ken's *father's* father had warned *him*, that the world was in peril of falling apart. The reason wasn't the threat of nuclear war or biological warfare. It wasn't communism or anarchy, although these were close. *No, the reason was society's family structure was eroding,* Ken thought as he donned his VR headset in the comfort of his suite. With one gourmet, in-house chef-prepared dinner of premium steak and two glasses of wine down the hatch, he was primed and ready to see how he could use the little incel dweeb. *Gay marriage, polyamorous marriage,* he thought as he went through Ty's introduction with all the enthusiasm of a snail. *Good thing the president has the Supreme Court primed to shut all the bullshit down.*

Ken related to Lester how, for the men in Ken's family, the trouble all began when women were allowed to own property and vote, never mind the access to abortions and birth control that would come decades later. The squabbling of one hundred years' time, as far as Ken's all too opinionated uncles and cousins saw it, had imperiled the future of their nation and fostered a wanton culture of depraved lunatics who worship mental illness and thrive on the eradication of religion.

Upon hearing this, Lester perked up and felt a renewed hope inside, but then he squashed it back down. It was too early to have hope for the triumphant return of Man's world, especially so soon after Eric's fiasco.

"I can't give you access to the player records like you were hoping, but seriously, I want to help," Ken admitted. He then insisted, "There must be something else we can do, something concrete that can change the fabric of society." His voice was one of sure confidence.

Lester shook his head and tutted quietly, "We cannot change the system as it exists now, no more than we can change our God-given bodily systems."

"Yeah, uh, right, buddy," Ken scratched the back of his neck. "You know, some people just get plastic surgery."

"Superficial changes that can only yield superficial results," Lester maintained. "Besides, not everyone can get plastic surgery."

This was where he lost Ken, who was willing to feign a friendly smile and hold his tongue for now while holding on to a hope that the future Lester envisioned might be possible. He pictured having a harem of purchased wives that would await him at home, springing to his every need when he walked in the door. He had enough money for it, and then some. Enough to keep the wives all happy with kids that would fight for his attention. *Oh, the magnificent drama of it all*, he thought.

"So, what do we do? There's no chance you'll be able to hack into the Server again. After your little show, security is tighter than a witch's vag in a blizzard."

Lester didn't have a plan yet, but he had a horrible idea.

Feeling alive, Maxx drifted through the six-way intersection on the Milwaukee Virtua track and took off down North Farwell Avenue with a jolt of NOS. The streetlights flitted overhead, giving his bad temper a long overdue massage. The screech of peeling tires took him back to when he and his dad used to hot rod around town in the old Firebird. He grinned to himself as he clutched the steering wheel, drifted again. He and the old man used to get the cops called on them whenever the neighbors could no longer hear themselves say "exhibition of speed" over the sound of the engine. The father and son might have been partly to blame for LA drivers' having their manual driving privileges limited. It was as if that time of his life began to meld with the present, merging into the leather seats and the flash of five-thousand-dollar paint jobs that tried to pass him.

Some Unknown was neck and neck with him, knuckles tight, when Maxx pulled off a tight enough drift to fade into first place. The Unknown dumped their NOS injection and held on. In RL, they could all die horrifically doing this. But here, immortality made the racers bolder and the event more exciting. Maxx hit a straightaway, glimpsed the speedometer, read '220'. The blurred walls of empty city blocks screamed past. The two leaders were almost neck and neck again when in a small piece of Maxx's brain, not enough to account for any large part of his conscious mind, synapses fired which recalled the words of his father on a beautiful, cloudless summer day in 2038…

You're not a bulldog on a chain, son. Old Yemminy needs a chain when he goes outside or else he'd run amok. You go where you want, do what you want. Nobody can tell you otherwise as long as you don't hurt nobody, and if they try to, just remember this: sometimes you gotta' go against the grain, sometimes you gotta' go with the flow. Sometimes you're not gonna' know when to do which. Tough shit.

The Unknown viciously bashed into the side of Maxx's Firebird with his antique 1967 Camaro. Maxx fought to keep his wheels straight. Again and again the hefty Camaro bashed into him. The Firebird hopped and bucked with each aggravating collision. Much more of this and one of the cars was bound to flip, and it would probably be Maxx. Furious, he thought to shout at the driver through his driver-side window, but this would only make it more difficult to maintain control.

They roared on over the final stretch. The finish line was closing in. The rhythm of the Camaro's side-bashing had become predictable. Smashing into the side of Maxx's car one last time, the Camaro driver was caught severely off guard when Maxx let go of the steering wheel, leading to a sudden change in direction that caused both vehicles to spin out simultaneously as a pair, their sides gripping like Velcro. By the time they had turned two hundred and seventy degrees, Maxx finally laid his hands on the wheel, corrected his path. The tires beneath him shrieked, smoked, and gripped the road. The Firebird separated from the Camaro, which continued its chaotic spiral. Playing dirty had resulted in the Unknown falling out of the lead and into last place. When Maxx crossed the finish line, he felt the living memory that was the embodiment of his father deep inside his heart as he shouted and cheered just like the old man used to.

Back in Lester's room in RL, Ken was losing his patience. Hours spent discussing and brainstorming had revealed Lester's agenda, but still no concrete plan of action. The corporate bigwig that he was, he needed to see a more detailed vision than what they currently had. He sat on an unsteady rotating office chair in Lester's cave-like dwelling. There were holes in the seat cushions that Ken's lavishly expensive suit insisted he had no business sitting on. Lester paid this no mind. He was possessed by an idea, and he wouldn't quit until he explored every devious avenue.

"Video games. People loved them when they first came out, and they have ever since," Ken commented to nobody really, speaking for Lester to hear only if he really cared to. "Then again, they say some people were picked on for it. *Nerds,* such a lovely word. We could use that, don't you think?"

Lester heard him but wasn't listening. The physical side of his machine, which police allowed him to keep since no hacking charges had been filed against him, was not an issue, he decided. The tether was perfect, the helmet was perfect. The problem now was how to change the programming, how to alter the penetration interface that had allowed him to slip past the Server's gatekeepers undetected. Lester was hunched over, eyes fixed on his desktop screen. Ken looked around the garage for something to keep his mind occupied and saw three short aisles of shelving stacked with computer parts and components that were of mysterious origin to him.

"Hey, what are you working on over there?"

Lester pushed his keyboard away and sighed wearily, "I can't tell you that, *K*. You need plausible deniability, among other things. If we can't get those player records, then we'll have to get creative."

Ken spun his chair toward Lester, "I've got it! We go on a spending spree. Purge the aisles at every hypermarket of all condoms, make it so that people have to have unprotected sex or no sex at all."

Lester had been holding his eyes shut, but opened them when Ken finished his sentence, "Needs work, *K*. Keep going, what else?"

Ken, who was used to being the one to ask this question at high-stakes business meetings between international conglomerates, found himself on the other side of the fence, scrambling for an idea, "Well, um, yeah, um... we stage a boycott! Yeah! We boycott women-run businesses. We submit a bill proposal to our government representatives to have women's rights of possession taken away. No, wait..."

"I like the energy, but we need something that is within our reach. Something that will actually catch on. Something that's going to stick."

Lester's head swirled with fresh lines of computer code. He wanted to know how to penetrate the impenetrable. A fitting quest, he admitted to himself. Once inside, however, there still remained a number of problems. Security sweeps were likely more frequent and more sophisticated now, since the staff wouldn't have understood just how Lester had gained access to begin with, much less how he and Eric had manipulated the Server architecture in order to remain hidden. And the player records? To steal or not to steal? The records would likely be better protected now too.

"What if we spread the word in a more organic way. We organize, we start a group. If they won't accept our bill proposal, we'll organize protests. We block traffic. We do everything those lib-tard commies pull whenever they try to get their way. Fire with fire, what do you think?"

Lester suppressed an eyeroll as best he could. The old dichotomy Ken was going on about was bound to fail. He stared at the particleboard wall where he pinned up his offline ideas. The notes would be unintelligible to most people. Ken didn't even try to understand them. *Magnitude Rectification. Curling Iron War. The Domestication of Women. Fits for Tits. Familial Irrationality.* It may have been a roadmap of his thoughts, but the fact remained that the vast majority of the country disagreed with him, which made him wonder whether all these ideas were doomed to fail. Pouring years of his life into developing the perfect technology to infiltrate Virtua's digital headquarters had all been for nothing. If years of dedication in developing a technology could not further his vision, a technology deemed to be the most sophisticated in the world as per Ken's astonishment, perhaps nothing could. Perhaps vengeance was a lost cause. Perhaps he himself had been the fool all this time.

"I'm trying my best, kid. I'm an idea person for a living, a very gainful living I might add, so you ought to consider listening to me," Ken's voice had returned to its initial tone from when he first encountered Lester in the interrogation room. Lester's face and chest got hotter than the contents of a crucible. Waves of heat flushed through him. This man, this *Ken the Suit* was the chaddest of all the chads, alpha male trying to tell the incel how to live, the same old game. Lester was hoping to get more use out of the Suit despite this, that alphas and incels could somehow join forces and end the sexual pyramid scheme once and for all. Maybe this was just another in his long list of mistakes.

"Actually... tell me more, K."

"It's Ken..."

Liz and the squad were amped to the max. The race had been closer than close, with Maxx battling for first place practically the entire time. After each of his friends was eliminated one by one, Observer Mode allowed them all watch the race in its every heart-stopping moment, every turn and crash. When Maxx stepped out of his ride and approached them, they all jumped, cheered, and hugged him. Only *Errigo,* who smiled and applauded exuberantly, stood apart from them. For the first time, Maxx smiled at Eric warmly.

"What did you think of that, Errigo? Did you like those moves?"

"That spin at the end was grand. How did you do that?"

"Got to know when to push and when to be pushed."

Eric thought he might have understood this but wasn't sure. While everyone else fawned over their champion, Candy was growing restless and fidgety. Her and Eric slowly started a conversation about how the race had unfolded. Some of the racers never had a chance. Others had formed a continuous stretch of competing drivers while Maxx and his rival spent the whole race at the forefront. Candy tried to contain herself. She was eager to usher everyone away to the next videogame selection, which was to be her choice.

Maxx soaked up the love. He needed a win like this, not that he'd ever admit to it. Not long had passed since he lost his father, the most steadfast figure in all his life, the one who stood by him and supported him when Maxx's husband divorced him and broke his heart. Despite an initial phase of trying to tell his son that homosexuality was wrong, Maxx's father had grown to learn oceans about humanity, both his own as well as humanity at large. The unyielding support that followed in after years, that loving embrace that did not flinch when a yearning for his father pushed Maxx to reach for a hug, it was gone now.

Of course, he told his friends when it happened, and of course they were always there with shoulders to cry on, but he never cried. In fact, it was apparent to the whole crew that he had never really grieved, not from what they could tell. Inside, they hoped that this was because in his stoic way he'd accepted his father's death unquestioningly and was perhaps handling it better than any one of them could have.

After waiting an appropriate amount of time for the champion to take in his glory, Candy conspicuously cleared her throat, then butted in. "All right, all right. We all love Maxx. Can we get a move on now, please?"

"Okay, you guys go ahead. I'm going to take break," Maxx added, followed by Liz and Sam's protest that he should stay on for a while longer. "I'll be back soon. I just need to hit the bathroom, eat, rest my eyes, and I'll be right back. Have fun steam fishing!"

Steam Fishing was Candy's favorite game because it allowed her to escape the highly digital world around her and slip into an older time, that is, the steampunk time. She reflected on the irony of escaping the computerized world while playing a computer game. Just over one hundred and twenty years since the start of the space age, and computer screens now appeared in every possible human interaction. When getting into an Otto, you don't swipe a card or pay with your phone any more – you interact with a screen, then lasers scan your eyes for DNA. When you stop in front of your refrigerator to do a little shopping, you use a screen to order your selections, and the robot that arrives at your door has a screen for a face. School through a screen, events through a screen. People did still meet up in person, but it was becoming increasingly rare. Even the bar scene, once celebrated worldwide, saw numbers taper off as people began to prefer private events with friends and family.

Yes, there were crowds that held on to the older ways, but facts were facts – only about five percent of people attended concerts in person any more. It was more of a thing for older people. The older someone was, the more likely that they still went to live concerts or live theater. Now the VirtuaHelm™ was changing it all. Younger people celebrated the safety VR afforded them – safety from random mass shootings, pandemics, assault and so on. And yes, many bemoaned this new reality. *Younger generations choose safety over living* was the general tone of several headlines.

"Why would you want to go back to a time when women couldn't vote or even own property?" Liz couldn't understand

Candy's steampunk fascination. To her and most revolutionaries, the Victorian Era represented nothing more than shameless imperialism gone off the rails.

"It isn't like I really want to live in that time. I mean I'm curious, *but no*," Candy said as she fiddled her tail with her forepaws. "I'm just fascinated with the reality that those people lived, how different their lives were from ours and how in such a short amount of time things changed so much."

Liz had a response for her immediately, "A short amount of time? Seems to me that a lot can change in two hundred years."

Candy didn't argue the point. She wasn't one for argumentation. She saw things a certain way and didn't bother to explain why. Eric noticed this, and he felt he understood. Candy could just have easily accepted that Liz was right, ignore her own feelings, but she chose to simply back out, no final word needed.

Liz went on for a time, complaining about how people romanticize the past when in the end all of history was a crime. Candy handled this with an almost regal tolerance, Eric thought as they made their way to the portal that would take them to Candy's favorite game. Sam flicked an aggravated look at Liz to get her to drop it already. At last Liz experienced a touch of self-awareness and gave it a rest. She never meant any harm, but she was always one to put something down if she thought it was stupid. It didn't matter who or what it was.

They arrived at the portal, which was located a fair distance beyond the edge of Prium in an old, abandoned train station. Next to the station ran a short length of track, as if left behind purely for touristic purposes. Long fissures ran through and divided fibers in the boards of aged, desiccated wood that sided the building. Liz issued one final complaint,

"Why do they make us come so far? Can't even teleport out

here."

Candy turned an unannoyed face to her friend, "That's the point. We're going to a place and time where the limits of technology were much more severe than they are today, so the long journey to get there is a part of the experience."

"Right. Otherwise it would be like teleporting to the end of a wagon ride. You'd miss all the colorful leaves if you didn't slow down long enough to look at them," Sam offered. Liz kept quiet, discontent with the logic but deciding not to argue any further. The station door creaked when Candy opened it and flooded the dark interior with a sunbeam. A mirror on the far wall, upon being struck by this light, caused some unseen mechanism behind it to sink. The switch must have been contained within a narrow, cylindrical chamber. There was then a whirring noise which caused the secret door to open slowly, emitting a clatter of cold gears. Metal on metal. Candy was thrilled. Neither Sam, Liz, nor Eric could deny that this was indeed fascinating. What could be behind the door?

Their transition into the subserver was completely unnoticeable as they all crossed into the darkness beyond the threshold of the wall. An antique filament bulb clicked on at the tug of an NPC who appeared and acknowledged the crew with a nod, then asked, "What's the password?" The severe woman dressed in black stood beside the faintly buzzing lightbulb.

Candy assumed a comparably severe face and answered, "Collywobbles."

With the gravitas of an executioner, the woman threw a lever, and the whole squad found themselves in sudden freefall. As they descended, the blackness around them dotted with the occasional passing of seemingly random objects. A grandfather clock, its pendulum swinging. A typewriter, its keys striking a page as if some ghost were writing a novel. A horseshoe. A cannon. Shifting piles of rope. Candles, their wicks remarkably aflame.

When Eric realized he was no longer falling, but lying on a floor of tightly bound logs, he sat up and called out to his friends. All at once they called back, but from scattered directions. A flash of lightning peeled away the darkness and revealed the gameplay arena.

A brooding herd of dark clouds pervaded the sky. Some fifty yards across rocky ocean waves, Eric's friends all stood on their own log platforms, each as wide as a schooner. The waves jostled the platforms woefully. Candy's voice carried over the roar of the storm, but only just. "The steam-fish try to knock us into the water, and when they do, we try to nail them with our cannons. If you fall into the water, swim back as fast as you can or else the steam-fish will eat you, and the crew inside will hold you captive until the game is over. Keep your heads on a swivel!"

Liz struggled to keep a steady base, nearly falling off the platform before she managed to gain her sea legs. When she reached the cannon and found the firing mechanism, she had seconds before the first steam-fish broke the surface directly in front of Candy's platform. Not reacting quickly enough to shoot the mechanical beast when it broke the water, Candy cried with glee and fired three successive misses. Eric and the rest fired too, all missing.

"Watch the surface for engine bubbles!" Candy yelled.

These impossibly nimble submarines looked like scrap-metal sculptures of something between a shark and an orca. Silvery gray and lined with rivets, the mechanical beasts had frontend grates in the shape of jagged-toothed mouths from which the underwater steam engine's exhaust poured out, filtered

103

by the cold ocean water. Black smoke trailed behind them like capes as five more chaotically broke the surface. These weren't NPCs – they were player characters who had been waiting for their chance to take on a group of challengers. Deep inside the machines the pilots wiped the simulated heat of the engines from their brows and licked their salty lips.

One unfortunate steam-fish pilot took too high of an angle and got slammed with one of Candy's next cannon shots, instantly rendering it a fireball with a spray of shredded metal. The surprise combined with an immediately subsequent jump caused Sam to lose xyr footing just as one steam-fish streamed in at an extremely low angle, almost removing xem from xyr platform in a swift motion. Candy screamed bloody murder, to the hilarity and hyena laughs of all.

"SAM!" Candy went full Rambo and fired shot after shot, reloading her cannon twice as fast. "You dirty sons of bitches!"

Eric laughed hysterically, so much that he was no longer able to reload his cannon and fell to one knee. An expertly aimed fish swiped him off the platform, and the next thing Eric knew, he was on a rickety conveyer belt that slowly drew him down into a room with a dim red glow. The conveyor stopped with a hiss, and Eric lifted his head. It was the engine room of the steam-fish.

"Just take it easy and make yourself comfortable or I'll have to put this thing in park, and you don't want me to do that."

Eric noticed a black, pixie-haired individual smeared in grease and sweat wrestling with the rudimentary controls of the machine. She didn't bother turning back to stare him down. She didn't have to. Eric assumed the heavy-duty wrench hanging in one of her belt loops could be used to equalize any contrary situation. He considered putting this to the test. What did he have to lose?

"Some people think they can take a shot at me and I won't see it coming. Word of advice: if you're one of those people, aim carefully."

Eric scanned the room. No blunt objects, no projectiles. He would have to tackle her. He remembered Candy's euphoric cries of feigned desperation. Make-believe. Pretend. Imagination. He sprinted towards the pilot and tackled her away from the controls. The two of them rolled across the floor and Pixie Hair wound up on top. Eric would have told her that he wasn't giving up without a fight, but, with an arm straight and strong as an iron bar, she held a comically large-barreled pistol to his forehead and spoke first, "Shouldn't have done that."

Eric's first fatality. He didn't hear the pistol shot. Instead, he suddenly felt an air of penetrating calm. Everything took on a shade of blue. Pixie Hair returned her gun to its holster and went back to wrestling with her controls. Sounds echoed as if far away, and this at last made Eric realize that he was in Limbo, the kind of semi-death observer mode that temporarily kicked players out of the game. He swore and complained that Pixie Hair had gotten lucky, even if she had clearly bested him. She was still in the game, so she couldn't hear him.

Eric wanted to know how the squad was fairing, so his ghostly avatar shot up through the steam-fish and the twenty meters of water above it, up higher still until he was floating over the field of play. The sight of the clouds and waves was so breathtaking that he momentarily forgot where he was and what he was doing. Yeah, that first time in Limbo is incredible. Squares of digital light that seemed both far away and part of Eric's eyeballs displayed the names and stats of all players on the subserver. The storm's bursts of lightning were dulled in their explosive sound, their glow subdued by the blue of Limbo.

After watching Liz's health gauge take a sudden dive, Eric reached out and touched her profile square, instantly transporting himself to her side. One of the steam-fish had knocked her off the platform, and now her pants leg was caught in the metal jaws of the machine. As it was being pulled deep below the surface with great force, her upper body trailed through the current as Eric's Limbo-spirit panned along with her, unfazed by the environment.

Her fate now inevitable, Eric's concern with Liz's oxygen meter running out subsided. Above the surface, the steam-fish broke the water again and dove at Sam. Eric could hear xyr scared yell in reaction. Xe had initially managed to not-so-gracefully dodge the vessel without falling when Liz was de-platformed. Eric tried to stifle his laughter at first, then burst out when he remembered that no one could see or hear him in Limbo, although it appeared Liz and Sam would be joining him soon. Sure enough, Liz appeared at his side, her oxygen meter having finally petered out.

"What a freaking rush!" She was breathing hard. "After Sam! Come on!" She grabbed Eric's hand and jumped toward Sam's square. The two crossed into hyper speed, rapidly traversing the playing field. Sam was in the water now too! There was a blur of passing matter as the duo panned through the depths, which weren't half as cold as they would have been in RL.

Errigo asked, "Do you see xem?"

"No wait... there!" Liz thrusted out her finger to indicate a trio of circling steam-fish. Their bear-trap mouths belched plumes of smoke that wobbled to the surface, imprisoned in upward trains of bubbles. Kicking and punching at the water around xem to no effect whenever one of the machines came close, Sam did not look like xe would last long. This made being in Limbo difficult. Eric and Liz both wanted to help Sam but were unable to even encourage xem. They floated and circled the unfolding scene with a pained fascination.

Cannon balls streamed down one after the other, trailing ribbons of disturbed water. Candy was the only one left on a platform, and now she was trying not to be the only one left in the game. Two of the steam-fish were circling her now, homing in while she tried to save Sam. She could see that one was clearly larger than the rest, which meant that it held a crew of two instead of one. Skimming along the surface just close enough to break the water, a gunner popped out from the top of the machine and took a long, careful aim with a harpoon. A submarine with a harpoon. Surely their intention was to drag her down until Limbo took her. *Not a chance,* she thought.

The harpoon looked like pure Gothic mania come manifest. Elegant, deadly and intricately engraved, the harpoon flew from a six-foot barrel with a ring of cold steel. Candy had the spirit of *The Matrix* in her though, and would have done Keanu proud. Witnessing her dodge a perfect shot as if she had predicted the harpoon's exact path demoralized the shooter, who met his end abruptly when Candy recovered from her dodge with a backflip dismount off the cannon base, slapping the trigger the instant she stuck her landing. This shot sank the steam-fish, sending the shooter's partner into Limbo right along with him.

Errigo had panned up from the bottom to watch Candy in action and was rewarded with a stunning show. Here was this woman, so strong and in her element. She yelled and taunted and fired her cannon, still the albino ferret, still red-eyed crazy with love and spice and zest for life, cussing and raving. Majesty didn't describe it, comedy couldn't encapsulate it. It was wild, free, messy, and Candy was the guest of honor. Her body dysmorphic disorder did not define her. Eric, not Errigo, was moved at this so much that he secretly cried to himself, withholding any audible sobs should Liz or the others hear.

Here in Limbo, he could cry, and no one would see his blurred, ghostly tears. He could cry and not be asked what was wrong or be told to be strong. He could cry because he had seen something beautiful, and it reminded him that he too loved life after all.

Sam's howl filled the air and jolted Eric out of his silent tears. Down in the water, Sam had somehow managed to grab hold of one of the steam-fish as it made its approach for attack. Seeing xem just in time to stop herself from unloading a deadly cannon shot on the oncoming fish machine, fiery and terrifying though it was, Candy dove out of the way, losing her cannon in the process, which was quickly gobbled up after being knocked clear from the platform by the machine. Before the steam-fish could crash and destroy itself in the process, Sam threw xemself and landed harshly on the platform. Bursts of incandescence rocked the waves, displacing the ocean water and the platform with it. Three steam-fish remained.

"I thought you were a goner!" Candy exclaimed.

Sam answered, "My oxygen bar almost ran out." Xe sputtered the feeling of real water away from xyr face. "They got the cannon. What are we going to do?" To Sam, there didn't appear to be any solution, but the game hadn't been won yet and they hadn't set a time limit.

"Time to pull a Verónica…" Candy spoke softly.

"A what?"

Feeling inspired by Sam's maneuver, Candy hunched over and slammed a speed-increasing soda pop. She curled her polecat spine into a twisted stance, a coil ready to spring, and drew a dagger. The breaking of the water was their only signal, and when the exhaust-spewing jaws bore down on them, Candy jumped, spun, caught hold of the mechanical beast's spiky metal fin, and rode it down into the water.

Seeing this without quite believing it, Sam erratically wandered along the edge of the platform to search the waves. Peering down and nearly falling off, xe retreated to the middle and waited, doing what xe could to keep from losing xyr footing again. Then another steam-fish lunged, slid across the platform and ended Sam's thrilled, defiant scream with a chomp.

The last of the squad was being pulled deeper and deeper into the yawning oceanic pit below. In RL Candy would have been quickly crushed to death by the pressure. She found the vessel's hatch and opened it thanks to the lacking reality of water pressure, causing the otherwise very real water simulation to flood into the submarine. Entering, sealing the door behind her, and kicking the pilot into the burning coals of the steam engine, Candy ignored the thrashing, bugged-out 3D model left over from the player's death, a pilotless shell burning in the coals, and assumed the controls.

It was two against one now. In the control room, the ghostly Limbo occupants that were Candy's friends surrounded her, cheering invisibly as she engaged in a marine dogfight with the other vessels. It was a whole different game now, one that required torpedoes rather than cannon fire. That suited Candy fine. She preferred piloting the steam-fish and would take it over the platforms any day. Hijacking a steam-fish was a difficult task, one she rarely pulled off.

Exchanging torpedoes, darting and banking, each of them growing tenser by the second, the steam-fish tied knots in the water. Loop after loop, the vessels came closer to striking until

109

finally a single well-placed torpedo took the opponents out for good. The Squad had won! For a brief moment before they phased out of the subserver arena and into the chatrooms, everyone in Limbo materialized in the steam-fish with Candy, and they all celebrated and laughed in a splendid delirium.

Eight

"I say we let Candy pick again," Sam suggested, still laughing. They had all been impressed, even Liz, who took back everything bad she ever said about steampunk. Candy accepted this amicably without rubbing it in too much. Everyone was decided that, when it came to multiplayer games, Candy had the best taste, so they left the subserver to see what other trouble she might be able to get them into. Sam retold the story a few times about getting swallowed whole and chomped up in the fish machine in a blaze of glory. Eric asked Candy for pointers on how to aim better in that particular game as opposed to others.

Candy went on explaining this when Liz interrupted her, "Just got a message from Maxx. He's logging back on for a while. Says he's down for whatever game Candy picks." They were all happy to hear this news, then wondered what Candy's next choice was going to be.

Sam asked, "What's next? A puzzle game? Who doesn't love a little roleplay? RPGs are my favorite. Or maybe a survival game? Adventure? A rhythm game?"

"Ooo," Candy cooed and shook her furry hind quarters. "You said the magic word. My feet are all happy after that last victory. *Vive La Dance* it is!"

Once they were back in Prium beneath all its spaghetti-noodle bridges and neon lights, they realized that the next portal was not so close, so they decided to teleport. The experience of

111

teleportation was memorable enough. It reminded Eric of Limbo, but quicker, cleaner, and still blue, but without the feathery traces of mist. It wasn't instantaneous, rather it started with a twist of motion toward the destination. Objects, streets, and people were all smeared and stretched like blue paint on canvas. The party of friends then appeared before their desired portal.

One of Virtua's designers must have thought it would be fun to put a portal on a moving target, in this case literally a track on which a car would circumnavigate a round plaza somewhere near Prium's city center. Steps led up from a central circle to a raised perimeter that one had to ascend in order to jump into the portal, which moved with considerable speed but not so fast that you had to have a running start to make it through in time before it passed. The squad arrived near the edge of this circular plaza known as Tanzen Plaza, and Liz, their longtime leader, walked ahead with a formidable gait. When she slammed into the invisible wall, it hurt.

"Fucking *OW!*" Liz wasn't happy. "The hell is this shit, man?"

"You all right?" Eric asked. The friends recoiled from the plaza threshold and flocked over to Liz.

"I will be when I find out who put that there!" She watched the portal as it eased by on its track. There wasn't the slightest hint of a wall, yet it felt like her nose had gotten bopped with a ballpeen hammer.

"Let me see here…" Eric reached out and made like he was walking in the dark. When he touched the force field or whatever it was, it felt ice cold and wasn't slippery. In fact it didn't feel much like anything. Eric thought to describe it as solid air. Clearly this thing had been constructed for the sole purpose of keeping people out.

Her nose still sore, Liz immediately connected to Server Chat and opened a customer service ticket. Maxx joined Eric in feeling the wall, and together the two of them determined that it enclosed the entirety of the Tanzen Plaza, with no evidence of holes or other means of bypassing the cold, solid nothing.

"What do you think it could be?" Sam asked. Xe wanted to burn some time while they waited for Server staff to arrive.

"Maybe they're doing maintenance on the subserver and this is their way of keeping us from intruding on their work," Liz replied as she sat and nursed her throbbing schnozz. "But you'd think they could just turn the portal off for a while, right? They wouldn't let us walk straight into that thing. They'd color it or something, add a texture."

"Maybe that's what they wanted to do, but there's been some kind of a glitch," Sam offered. "Whatever it is, it's super weird. Like, a lot of weird stuff has been going on lately. No one ever found out what happened to that Runsdeep guy either. Virtua isn't saying anything. It's like he dropped off the face of the world map."

Maxx and Eric continued their search, unwilling or perhaps unable to let it go. Maxx in particular did not like to be bested. A sore loser all his life, he would exhaust every possibility before admitting defeat. Eric, on the other hand, had a lady to impress. They took turns at running starts to see how high up the wall went. They tried running up it, jumping off the last gripping step and slapping their hands along the side of the wall, finding no top, no end to it. Maxx could get a lot higher than Eric, but, wanting to be thorough, Eric kept trying in different places as well.

"You think they covered it up, sympathized with him? They said he was an incel fanatic or something, didn't they?" Sam asked.

"Don't you remember that little chat I had with him? Fuckin' *Runsdeep*. What the hell is that even supposed to mean? Virtua's never shown any signs of being that backwards, but we shouldn't put it past them. Who knows what they're capable of? One thing I know is we're starting a petition, like, now."

Sam didn't share Liz's enthusiasm, and this showed on xyr face, "You know, they... ah, never mind."

"What? Tell me."

"No, forget it."

"Hey! C'mon! Out with it."

"If they were guilty of covering anything up, do you think that a petition is really going to do anything?"

"Look at it this way: even if it doesn't do anything necessarily, it'll be in the public eye, and the more people we get to sign, the more Virtua looks like a bunch of assholes when they turn us down." Liz tried to mock-chant as if she were at a protest,

"We demand to see the man – charge Runsdeep, give us a peep... at his face!"

Sam paused, allowing the moment to dangle. "That'll convince them."

A lone Server agent appeared with a gentle cascade of sparks as though a golden waterfall had briefly fallen from nowhere, pulling her down with it. The woman who stood before them wore casual T-shirt and jeans. While her ears and brow were studded and skewered with an array of multi-colored piercings, some chrome, her body gave off a slight golden aura – the defining characteristic of an agent. Agents, like Monitors and Admins, held significantly more power than players, although agents were the lowest in the hierarchy of Server management.

"Agent Sara Adleman here to address ticket 40722111A-3.

What seems to be the problem?" The exceptionally tall woman had the posture of a proud professional eager to do good work. Sam liked her right away. Liz on the other hand still had a sore nose.

"I'll tell you what the problem is. I'm walking along here, right, minding my own business, leading my friends into the plaza when *WHAM!*" Liz clapped her hands together, which got a slight jump out of Agent Sara. "Face sandwich. Crushed my friggin' nose. Have a look at this thing…" Liz called over, "Hey, Maxx! Show her what all the fuss is."

Eric and Maxx gave a full demonstration. First they attempted to roll under the wall. Then they tried walking around it or through it. They even tried to jump over it, then invited the agent to try for herself. She confirmed its impenetrability in short order, and her face scrunched up in bewilderment.

"Calling Server Admins, Emergency Code Alpha Zeta One Five Ten. Calling Server Admins. We have an obstructive anomaly at Tanzen Plaza. Calling all Admins."

There was no queue, no wait time. Two balls of light swooped down from somewhere unseen and dissipated into a shimmery mist which coalesced and formed the ethereal, god-like bodies of the Admins. Sam and the gang could tell that something was definitely wrong, because a ticket never escalated straight up to an Admin unless something completely batshit crazy was going down. There was no sparing of pomp among the two Admins, who were clothed in long robes that draped beneath them as they floated through the air. The ridiculous sound of distant strings playing heavenly chords accompanied their presence. Both tried to speak at once.

"Wh–"

"Wh–" they began and stopped, then began and stopped

again, failing to cease interrupting each other until one finally powered through angrily.

"What is this? Who did this?"

The second Admin walked straight up to the barrier and laid his body and face against it out of a slavish fascination as would a socially depraved lunatic reaching out for a hug. "Who erected the wall?"

Everyone except the first Admin was weirded out by the second one's display. Eric finally answered, "Our friend Liz here walked straight into it. The wall has pain programed into it too, somehow, so you'll want to check that out... Wait a minute, how did you know the wall was there?"

The second Admin looked up at the invisible structure, which, in his eyes, reached forever into the sky.

"The Admins see all..." His voice was subdued, reverent, and thoroughly creepy. The second Admin still had his right cheek pressed against the cold nothing. Eric wondered whether they were in their right minds.

At last Agent Sara asked, "Can you see anything else? Is it only the wall?"

"It is a cylinder, rather, one that stretches up to the highest limits of space on the Server. The portal appears to have been heavily tampered with as well. We won't be able to tell exactly what we're dealing with until we start running tests."

Admin Two left the wall, face numb from the cold, and rushed over to Liz and the gang. He spoke so quickly that they could barely understand him, "Away! Aw-wa-away! Leave this place! We must convene! Yes..."

Admin One swayed and became very solemn, joining Admin Two in a bizarre ritual and chant in which they both hopped in a circle on one leg. This made absolutely no sense to the squad,

116

who lingered for a few seconds before awkwardly vacating the area. Liz gestured for them to follow her into a stone nook tucked within the corner of two city buildings. Once inside, she hissed a whisper, "This is that Runsdeep's doing, I just know it. You saw the look on that Admin's face. I know they're both batty as hatters, but that guy was spooked. Two days in a row, some hacker makes changes to the Server that were thought to be impossible."

Eric fought hard not to scratch that itch at the back of his head. It would have been too obvious. A dead giveaway. That's what he told himself. *Don't give yourself away. Don't give yourself away.*

Lester hummed a chuckle, pleased with himself. *Yes sirree.* The chad Ken had to go back to his fairytale world for a while, but said that he would return, and that when he did he expected Lester to have put their plan into action. Despite all his annoying alphamaleness, Lester couldn't help but find the man to be admirable in some way. Fully aware of his inceldom, Lester knew he was prone to both hate and envy the chads of the world. Another circumstance to which he fell victim as a man.

Ken would be disappointed when he got back, for Lester had a whole different plan up his sleeve, including what to do with the chad when he, or *it* came back. The wall was in place, the portal had been hijacked and carved out, bored deeper and wider than before to make space for Lester's magnum opus, his Men's Only section in a place where sexy women would flock to dance, sexy women he could never have, never love, never exploit. Entry, if it was ever to be allowed, would be to men only.

Lester imagined designing his own security, being his own Admin of his own subserver. *Vive La Dance is no more,* he thought to himself as he ambled through his new lightless, cavernous space where disco balls and music once dazzled the night. It wasn't a coincidence. This was to be a fitting last stand, the location being one he'd selected after extensive consideration and research of Eric's queer friends. And it was one of Candy's favorite games.

Candy had logged off and was now in her bedroom at home, no longer the fun-crazed ferret. Here in RL, what escape from body image did she have? Of course her fears came more strongly into focus, but tonight it was Liz who triggered the waves of self-loathing.

Not that she had meant to, and Candy wasn't sure why, but Liz's fury had brought her horrible past experiences with body image to mind. Normally Candy would enter into a frenzy right along with Liz, but tonight the memory of her own pain overwhelmed her. She needed to be alone despite her friends' insistence she stay at their sides. She pulled off the VirtuaHelm™ and cried in her bed for half an hour. After some time passed she started looking at herself in the mirror. Accepting her body was a peace that forever escaped her.

Pinned up on the wall next to her mirror was a hand-drawn picture of her furry online persona. Her alter ego's name, *Candy,* was written in pretty bubble cursive beneath a matching screenshot, with a little button heart shape dotting the letter *i* in the words *i love Candy.* When she read the name, she thoughtfully shook her head without loving it any less.

Candy's real name was Robyn.

Back on the Server, Liz pressed on. "We can't just sit and do nothing. We need to find another way in. We've got to make this fucker pay!"

Maxx was done. He decided to call it a night and said his good-byes in a hurry. He wasn't interested in feeding into Liz's frenzy, not even when she insisted that he stay up late with her online to work out the perfect plan.

Sam followed suit soon after. Liz received an external message from Candy saying she was going to stay offline for the night. Eric decided that now needed to be the time. He had to confess his experiences with Lester to Liz.

Nine

The walls of grainy, porous concrete in Lester's latest hideout groaned and gradually expanded. At the points where their corners and vertices met, a mush glooped out as if from nowhere, hardening into fresh wall. The walls appeared to be breathing. Lester continued setting up the base of operations in his stronghold with Ken, who had arrived only minutes earlier.

High-level Virtua staff had apprehended and remerged several of Lester's other lairs back into the primary network, and so much of what Ken had put away to make room for the pirate architecture had already been reabsorbed by the Server. Ken began losing patience with this apparent contraction the second he learned of it.

"I'm putting my foot down," he declared. "If none of my ideas are actually going to be put to use, maybe I need to follow through with my original plan and press charges, have the courts throw the book at you and your sick little incel buddies."

Little? Sick? Something snapped inside of Lester.

"Well, now that you mention it, K," he paused and waved one hand as if to shoo the words he'd said away, "I'm sorry – *Ken*, I have thought about it very carefully."

"Uh-huh."

"And I've decided to do things by the book this time. Let's form an organization like you said. Draft a bill proposal, use the democratic system of our great country to further our cause."

Ken was skeptical. You can't play a player, outfox a fox, or out-snake a snake. Ken had power in his hands, substantial influence over Virtua's PR campaigns and media, and legal interests in collaboration with the company's team of lawyers guaranteed that he could do whatever he wanted with Lester now. It was a familiar level of power to Ken, an aspect of being entirely in his element, or so he believed, and he wouldn't have had it any other way. Not if he could help it. Lester kept his head low and quietly invited Ken to follow him out of the main cavern and into a room he'd constructed in a small expansion into a wall. He promised it was going to be the first of many offices through which they would eventually conduct their world-changing business of spreading the incel word.

"You betas are good at organizing, I'll bet," Ken offered snidely with a condescending tone, his once amicable smile now crooked. Lester's torso stiffened, but he remained silent. Leading Ken into the tight chamber, he turned on a viewing screen and closed the door behind them. The soft white glow of the screen had made Ken feel safe enough to walk into the hole in the wall.

"I could fit ten of these in my office…" he began, then trailed off as Lester disappeared in an audible blip of a teleport. Ken quickly discovered there was no doorknob. In fact there wasn't any discernable way to open the door whatsoever. He was trapped.

Scared and alone, he pounded the wall and screamed every obscenity he'd ever heard in his life. When Lester's face appeared on the screen, Ken spun around to meet the voice that spoke to him, "You had to call me little, didn't you?"

"Let me out, you basic shit! You are dead, do you understand?"

"All in good time, little chad. You will notice that your log-

121

out capability has been disabled. One of the advantages to being the best hacker in all of California."

Ken's harshly infuriated face grew sharper as he slapped the back of his head with both hands and began to pull. No gesture recognition. No log-out screen. It was true. He wasn't getting out, and all his poise and composure crumbled at the realization.

Lester bid The Suit adieu and left him in the niche in the wall, where he would remain, screaming and alone, for a potential power play later on in the game.

Eric sat by himself in his kitchen without the usual despair in his heart. A thin draft of midnight air silently flowed in through the cracked window. Liz's reaction was no surprise. She was a progressive revolutionary and Lester was a man born a few hundred years too late. He was a homophobe, a misogynist, a narcissist, and if he really was as tech savvy as Eric described him to be, then he was a threat. Of course she was angry, and she needed to get away from Eric to process what she had learned from his story. Runsdeep99, it had been Eric!

RL was overrated, Liz thought, and tonight reminded her of that. She could plainly see that the city was a beauty, but who could fall in love with looks alone? Offline, standing on the Highway 1 bridge over the LA river, Liz took in the city noir and let her mind jostle with the thoughts. Errigo, who admitted that his name was actually Eric, had said that he learned his lesson, that he didn't want to be anything like Lester, that he had been confused and in pain, but could Liz really trust him now? The question lingered in her head.

She wasn't attracted to Eric. Not even a little, but she did think of him as a friend, and her crew of friends meant more to her than anyone or anything else. Nobody in her life was close to her like they were. Before the VirtuaHelm™ was released, they all used to meet up and play Grand Theft Auto or Final Fantasy. Other times they would play Agar.io and control little amoebas that would eat each other in order to grow until one became the largest. Then it was all about holding on to the lead as long as you could. Videogames were fun. They were awesome. Everyone needs a distraction. But what really kept her and her friends close were the moments in between, the small talk, the sharing. She thought back to when Eric first helped them take out the Chrome Tigers.

His voice echoed in her head, *Why do you have it out for these guys so bad?*

Eric had needed a convincing reason. When he found out it was personal, that the Chrome Tigers had hurt Candy's and Maxx's feelings, he didn't back down. Shy as he was, he didn't back out when they told him about the publicity surrounding their antics. Not even when they took on the POTUS.

Finally Liz pulled herself away from the vista and started her walk back home. High winds caught her hair. She had an idea on how they could make sure Lester wouldn't succeed in his plan.

Lester was at the top of his game. A smile that mocked the whole world would not leave his face. On the run, but still on a mission. *The Midnight Rider,* confident and cocky. Nobody could touch him. He'd nearly assumed the status of a chad, minus the sex. And yet, the power felt as good as he imagined sex must feel. Dispatching Ken had made him feel mighty. If society had been different, perhaps females would have taken notice, would have fawned over his success in defeating the alpha, embracing him as the new alpha. It was a guilty pleasure, imagining such a scenario, when for years he disdained those whose sexual lives he blamed to be ruining his.

After a couple of hours of Internet study, Lester determined the speed at which a human mind can come undone, and checked in with Mr. Alpha Suit Loser only after twenty-four hours. The mind of the man he found there was so changed that it disturbed Lester greatly, though not enough to prompt mercy. Waves of propaganda crashed in Lester's brain, propaganda he could issue out into cyberspace, flinging it into the darkest corners of the world. He could recruit them, start an army. They could form their own state. Secede from California.

There was a thud from deep within the now-disabled portal wall that shook Lester out of his dreamland. He scrambled to his feet, knocking over his fold-up chair in the process. *Stupid chair,* he thought, even though he had chosen this specific chair for a reason. As in so much in his life, he lived in protest of comfort, and the chair was yet another manifestation of that.

Another thud rocked the wall. This time he felt it in the floor and watched as dust and sand fell through dim lights from the ceiling above. *No. No.*

No no no no no FUCKING NOOOOO!

Liz, Eric, and the rest of the squad kept their aims centered on the unresponsive portal. The Admins had determined that it was directly linked to the hijacked Tanzen Plaza. Here, outside of Lester's final lair, they could tell nothing about what lie beyond the secret portal that he had erected in the flat rock formation beyond the perimeter of Prium. And yet the chance to end the terror here and now beckoned.

Eric smiled to himself, amused. Collaborating with the Admins on the compound assault had gotten him and the squad equipped with the finest weapons the Server could muster, virtual firehose-like devices known as *quills* that held the programming power to delete mountains and slurp up oceans. These God-mode weapons could be operated only by approved parties, which meant the squad could unload their focused streams of programming power without the fear of unleashing utter chaos upon the Server.

The Admins had been busy. Kooky, but busy. Using their arsenal of exotic and ultra-grade informatics resources, they quickly formed a compilation of snippets from conversations Lester had tried to have in secret over the years but which had nonetheless been picked up by NPC Monitors and background scanning. Several of the Admins expressed unabashed delight at the opportunity to push the capabilities of their monitoring software and problem resolution strategies so soon. They were unapologetically tickled. Liz worked closely with them after they noticed her and her squad's impressive win record, and thus their potential ability to help resolve the matter. She persistently reminded them that their own findings ruled the man to be a literal terrorist.

"Yes, yes, we understand, Liz," replied Admin Two, the one who had squished his face adoringly against the invisible wall when they initially found the anomaly, "but now that we've isolated the pathways of his pirated niche, he's got nowhere to go. There's no reason we can't have a bit of fun while we take care of business here."

"Listen to yourself!" Liz yelled over the hastening laser blasts that flashed from the end of her quill and struck the rock wall with bursts of sparkling incandescence. "This guy has evaded you for how long? How many times has he gotten away? You need to take this seriously."

"I assure you, we do take it seriously…"

Admin Two lost his train of thought and faded out of the conversation, bursting instead into a separate conversation with Admin One, who was at his side.

"Would you look at this! Incredible, truly incredible! He has once again expanded space within our parameters for space, creating his own *mini subserver*. Such amazing programming!"

Admin One nodded and smiled with equal enthusiasm. Liz felt sick.

Lester barricaded the structure of his niche as best he could. It was clearly a matter of time, judging from the sole camera feed that the Admins had purposely left open so he could watch his impending doom. *Eric and his band of freaks*, Lester screamed inward viciously. *Of course they're in bed with the almighty Admins!*

Hatred seethed within him as he alternated between pacing and drilling commands into his pirate interface, to zero effect.

I've come too far. It can't end here. Lester traced a long floating rectangle of red light. *I'm not going down without a fight, and if it's not going to be a fair fight, I'm not going to play fair either.* He traced another identical rectangle. Then another two. Then two squares. Trails of electrical arcs crawled along the edges of the glowing red prism and strayed over its surfaces in jutting forks. *Not one of them understands, not one! Who I must become now, the awful things that I must do – it's on them! Not me! I was not born a monster, I have been made into one! They'll see. I'll make them see!*

Lester tapped in his final programming command and stepped into the prism. Once inside and unseeable, he writhed through a sluggish, mud-laden sensation. His hacked avatar model Runsdeep1 merged with the Rundeep99 model, which he had created and intended for his treacherous disciple Eric, coalescing into a dangerous new form that rooted itself deep into Lester's brain.

Deep down into the core of his damaged psyche the avatar worked its billion tendrils and latched onto the source of Lester's fury, the gutter between his self-regard and the world around him. Years of studying his therapists' and collaborating cognitive scientists' notes led him to confidently isolate the parts of his brain that were most strongly associated with his constant feelings of rage. Certain memories and times in his life, the rejections, the experiences, the parts of his brain that adapted as a result. He stopped writhing and felt a gooey substance envelope every inch of him.

The substance hardened into body army of Lester's meticulous design – think one part *Venom*, one part *Iron Man*. Walking through the red prism, which faded into nothing once his body had exited it completely, Lester was no more. What remained was the very embodiment of everything that had plagued the man, his embracing of monsterhood, of misguided martyrdom. If he was to have no army, he would be a one-man army with nothing to lose.

Runsdeep waited for his attackers in the shadows of his encoded lair. Taking a peek in at the maddened Suit, he saw that the poor chad had stripped off all his clothes and was tearing them into long ribbons. Too bad. If Lester had known any mercy before fusing with the avatar, it was now gone.

Liz didn't care any more if the Admins were being dicks. She was pleased with their progress. Thanks to her collaboration with Server management, together they were gaining the upper hand.

The walls of the hacker's impressively coded niche were coming undone. Liz rallied her squad.

"Shock and awe, people, shock and awe!" She held on tight. The laser flashes were so rapid now that the quills had become machine guns spraying the waves of code into the portal. "We know the Server Admins are scanning for him, and we've got him pinned down. I say we call for reinforcements and stay here to make sure he doesn't get away. Eric, he can't hurt us, can he?"

"How could anybody hurt us in here?" Sam asked.

"I don't know. He's already done stuff that Virtua said was impossible on the Server. Well, Eric?" Liz wanted her answer now.

Eric shook his head, "From what I could tell he's just really good with gadgets and coding. I don't think we need to fear for our lives. He seems pretty harmless, to…," he hesitated, "…to be honest."

"*Harmless?*" Liz interrogated angrily and skeptically. "Harmless would be limiting his misery to complaining that girls don't like him. This guy's trying to screw with people, and if he really is a tech wizard genius, then we're all in a lot of trouble, aren't we?" She pressed them all with her eyes. Candy had a serious face. Sam was solemn. Maxx's brow could have cut through stone. "No, we need to bring this guy down, and we need to follow through to the end. Attend his trial, the works. We've got to see that he faces maximum sentencing."

"I don't think he's broken any laws really yet," Eric spoke cautiously, trying his best *not* to sound like he was defending the madman, "aside from the hacking."

"Still, I'm betting your testimony of his plans for the player records he was going to steal could get him in a heap of trouble, and that's what we should be aiming to do at this point, Eric," Liz retorted, trying her best not to sound like she was accusing him of protecting Lester. She didn't suspect him of that any more. Her fear was that he would naively fail to take the danger of Lester's philosophies and actions seriously. *Give these pricks an inch, and they'll get their conservative buddies to help normalize the bullshit. Before you know it, women won't be able to get credit cards any more, then things will get even worse.*

Liz widened her stance and doubled her resolve. The first layers of exposed coding malfunctions were beginning to unravel and burst like exploding tomatoes.

Ten

Runsdeep quickened his pace. He crammed a desperate series of mental programming commands through the Interface. There had to be a solution to this mess.

Pinned down in his self-contained niche with no access to the alternate exit in Tanzen Plaza, there was no logging out for the hacker any more. He was trapped in his own Faraday cage which had been a necessary feature to ensure no person or mechanism on the Server could delete his last bastion. He was going to lord his own private club over the rest of the Server, protected by his invisible wall. *It was going to be glorious.*

He had failed. The architecture of his niche wasn't indestructible after all. *Failure. My reality,* he thought, *my inescapable curse.* He clenched his jaw. It was supposed to be a Men's Only club. He was going to make members take blood tests to confirm that they carried the Y chromosome. *It was going to be glorious.* He seethed.

The Suit was braiding the torn ribbons of his high-end clothes into some kind of new garment, having taught himself the new skill during his many hours in isolation. Deep inside, Runsdeep felt a spark of the tiniest remembrance of what pity felt like when he saw this display, only for the spark to sizzle and burn out. He stretched, got as limber as he could, and started to sprint toward the portal wall.

"Focus in on him! Compensate the variable scanners. For Christ's

130

sake, people, look alive! There! Fire! No, there! Run! Execute!"

Admin One was livid. The hacker, having ultimately decided to commence the battle sooner than later, began to appear in blips just long enough to rock the outside world with the full force of an anti-air gun before disappearing again. In and out of the sinuous space between spaces he weaved, blanketed beneath the currents of unraveling code that churned about him like a maelstrom.

Reinforcements were beginning to arrive and were quickly grabbed by the backs of their necks and thrown into the fray. Unable to determine where he was going to reappear, most of the agents and Monitors unloaded their novel capture fields (lasers designed to isolate and trap the hacker's unique coding language) in random directions, pointing and dragging without success. It was the niche, the Server staff knew it was. That space between spaces was breaking all the laws of manageable coding, and if they didn't contain it and put an end to the chaotic breach between the Server and the artificial architecture, the chaos was going to spread.

Maxx wielded his quill defiantly when Runsdeep appeared in all his terrifying presence and gooey flesh. Monitors and Admins all turned their weapons, but Maxx had already been flung into the air, targeted by the terrorist's coding magic. Liz and the rest watched his body sail away into the sky and horizon after being annihilated by an awesome power which connected with the force of a hundred trains. They accepted instantly that he would not, could not have survived the gory injury, and unless they could bypass the Server's rules, he would fall into Limbo for twenty-four hours. The squad's first casualty, spectacularly defeated.

Eric fired into the air and managed to blast the hacker with one clean shot, but was punished with a round of explosive code that hammered him into the ground. He sank helplessly to the bottom of the resulting crater that was fifteen feet wide.

Eric's blast had nevertheless thrown Runsdeep off balance, and a volley of laser fire from the squad and management staff pinned him to the surface of the invisible portal, which quickly flourished around him with the brilliance of a spotlight. Missiles of coding packages were shot at him in massive gobs that stuck to his body, attacking the goo armor, trying to extract the man from somewhere deep inside.

There's still a human being beneath it all, Sam thought to xemself as xe focused the laser of xyr quill. This figure, part man, part machine, was suspended in a conflict within himself, seeking an answer that escaped him. Runsdeep cried frighteningly in the manner of a squeal, a bleat, a neigh, and a roar all at once and sank into the portal.

Ken was wearing a dress now. Having spared no attention to detail, the elaborate braiding puzzled Runsdeep when he appeared in the cell to check on the prisoner. Shit outside the hideout was hitting the fan, and now the chad, the alpha, was wearing a dress and dancing seductively, signaling with his finger for Lester to come out of his avatar and join him down on the floor.

This was having the desired effect. Deep down inside of the avatar, Lester turned and watched Ken's odd-yet-sexy tossing and turning on the floor, his twerking movements, and felt torn. He was ashamed, but The Dress shaking her little ass made him want to forget that Ken was a man, remove the dress, and engage in the act. Celibacy at Lester's age was a cruel joke so far as he was concerned. It was time to end it, wasn't it? *No!* Finally

Runsdeep slapped the command on his display screen and booted The Dress out of the cell and out of the coded niche for good.

Outside the niche, management staff were discussing their options for the final phase of dismantling the hacker's encoded barriers when Ken Faraday was ejected from the portal and fell harshly onto the ground like a sack of mushy potatoes. The maddened company rep got right up to his feet, and, with an unhinged cadence, started to babble nonsense that chilled everyone around him to their cores. "Howdy! Gobble-gobble! Tocks wound me up. Twisted the worst, wanted to, so bad! Heavens sing, I said," he persistently made uncomfortable eye contact with each and every gawking onlooker, "and it was a shower, a broken tip of a leaf blower, and I'll FUCKING PAUSE!" He screamed in a random agent's face, who recoiled and ran away.

Monitors tried to escort Ken peacefully, but he kept screaming his unintelligible rant, and swung his fists hard at anyone who tried to apprehend him, connecting with the heads of a few Monitors and then one of the Admins. Then they struck him with an energized green clump of immobilizing code and force-logged him out. Immediately a storm of debate reared up amongst the management staff who yelled and berated each other over who would be liable for the deranged man they just booted from the Server.

Lester scrolled through his various backup plans, found no alternative. This would have to be his last stand in this space between spaces, buried somewhere in the rock wall.

He readied his most sinister weapons, piles of hacking commands that would enable him to do some booting of his own, or rather reverse booting. Rivers of tears ran down his tired, pain-stricken face in RL, and he could just barely feel his cold, wet cheeks feeding back into the Server. He had long accepted life to be a waking nightmare from which only death would be an escape. Afraid to die and perhaps too stubborn to admit defeat, his mission to spread the word of his cause was the one thing that kept him going, like God for church people or drugs for addicts, or the mall for the mall-folk.

Maybe when you lose your virginity you don't need any of those things any more, but how would Lester know? *And what,* he wondered, paranoid and afraid, *am I supposed to turn myself in quietly, give up peacefully, be a good little beta and take it up the ass in a prison cell like I'm supposed to?* If anyone else could have heard these thoughts of his, any one of those trying to break into his niche, or any of his long-estranged family members, many would have been horrified. Rightly so, because it wasn't just frustration with involuntary celibacy any more. The enemy was anyone who got in his way.

One Monitor who had the professional attire and instructive tone of an enthusiastic high school teacher rounded up a number of volunteers among the onlookers who were fascinated with the situation. Their goal would be to pinpoint the exact location of the hacker's so-called niche, or pirated digital-spatial distortion. Liz and the squad took a breather and let the techies do their thing while the volunteers probed the wall to test the resistance of the barrier coding. She started to gripe about the danger that management staff were putting volunteers in, but gave it a rest when she saw Sam's face grow weary. Liz decided to let the others do the talking as they changed the subject to pass the time.

The wait was excruciating. Actively wondering whether

Lester would ever answer for his conspiracy was not an appealing way to await their next move. They talked about meeting in RL someday, all of them, going to a real beach somewhere and maybe even having a barbecue. Candy would do the cooking.

The Admins renewed their squabbling, "We need to focus the attack sequence *now!*" This Admin swiftly floated up above the rest like a super hero in order to draw their attention. "If Ash shows up and we haven't even set up the penetration patterns, we'll be babysitting robots in a factory by Tuesday."

The Admins continued their bickering for a short while before they started to shush each other into silence. Another Admin was descending from on high, looking much like a celestially-appointed lawyer with a panache for mischief. This wasn't just any Admin though. It was CEO Ashley Quinn Fournier.

"No more screwing around," the stately woman in a sharp, angular suit declared as she lightly touched the ground and strode toward Tanzen Plaza. "Let's gut this turkey."

The CEO's assistants buzzed around her as if she were a megacorp Snow White and they her forest friends. Ashley Quinn Fournier's superpowered armor, freshly designed by the company's top programmers, crawled up out of the container that one assistant placed before her. The sparkling, sinewy mass of flowing particles then did a snake's dance as it ascended from its vessel and wrapped around the legs of the already powerful CEO.

Upon making contact with her body, Ashley's eyes went white with true sight, and all the Server's streaming traffic of programming was revealed to her as it passed in every direction. The particles of the armor flowed like a liquid yet held their form like a solid, encasing the CEO in a formidable shell, a queen's angelic suit of armor imbued with more power than ever before unleashed upon Prium. Liz slammed a defense-increasing grape soda pop and looked on, inspired and starstruck.

What happened next took everyone off guard. Runsdeep appeared in a concussive boom that rocked everyone but the CEO to their knees. Furious at the prospect of so quickly losing a round to this pain in her ass, Ashley unloaded a blast of destructive power devised to obliterate the coding and modeling data of whatever it struck. Before the vast column of white, searing fury could terminate Runsdeep, the virus teleported itself and Eric back into its niche. The destructive beam annihilated what remained of Lester's barrier coding and exposed the face of the dormant portal, which he had locked. The lock would be no match for the Admins nor the CEO, who had time to spare.

It wouldn't be long before the security experts busted their way in. Beneath the awful goo of his viral armor, Lester knew that. There would only be one way out that he could accept – martyrdom. Beyond a doomed effort to isolate his enemies in the niche's prison cells where they would hopefully lose their minds like Ken, there was still a way to save face, to honor the blackpill cause.

"You will go down with me," the goo on Runsdeep's head and shoulders sizzled and popped like eggs in a pan as it spoke. "You will confess your own inceldom. We will have our stories told to the world, and all its media will dissect our vision, and the audience will grow and grow."

"Fuck off," Eric spat the hateful words.

"Not wise," Lester returned. Otherworldly sounds of the portal architecture being ripped to shreds rang throughout the niche hall, and a kind of fog leaked in from the walls like they were being cooked, yet everything was still cold. Eric sat in the murk, disgusted that he almost had almost become Lester, who wasn't even himself any more.

Eric spoke in a hushed voice, and Runsdeep drew near, "I don't care what you think. I'm not going to help you."

"You're going to tell them what that feminist void did to you," the virus declared.

"She just wasn't interested."

"No one ever is, are they? She had the power to end that. You blame her. It's her fault. Admit it."

"No it isn't!" Eric ran and tackled Lester, but his avatar enhancements made the tussle last all of one second. Piledriving him into the floor, Lester, or Runsdeep, wound up a punch as he uttered his last warning.

"Tell them. Tell them what she did, you coward!"

A section of wall was oozing out a fog that was much thicker than before when there was a sudden implosion of blinding light rays and flying debris. The glitchy chunks of rock wall, trimmed with strings of damaged, twitching graphics, flew and struck both Lester and Eric. Among the incoming boulders that were still in mid-flight soared the CEO, her army of management staff, Liz's squad, and an entourage of go-getter randos.

Recovering from the initial blow while Eric's avatar was nearly nullified, Lester pivoted his heel on a boulder behind him, and before any of the other boulders came near to touching the ground, Lester took hold of Eric and used him as a human shield against the oncoming rocks and sizzling blasts of code.

Had it been another day, the CEO and Lester's monstrosity might have been evenly matched. Had the two faced off mano a *womano*, maybe it would have been a good fight, but Ashley Fournier had an army, and Liz had an idol to impress.

Finally the airborne scene made contact with the floor, and

Eric felt the crushing weight of boulder upon boulder nailing him in the face and chest – minus the pain, but still disorienting. A righteous column of world-ending code-laser struck Lester at last when Eric wrestled his way free, and the man and his avatar froze. Pinned down by the dozens of Admins and their immobilizing rays, Lester was instantly subdued. He let loose a cry of impotent fury somewhere between a shriek and a squeal, disturbing all who heard it. Liz managed to stifle a wild cackle she felt coming on. Eventually the hacker's body went rigid, and he made no more sound.

Oozing into a puddle that gathered at his feet, the gooey black armor melted off of Lester. The man's human form lay prone, seemingly lifeless, unresponsive. The black ooze began to move of its own accord, forming limbs and pulling itself along like the agonized survivor of a horrible car wreck before being contained by the management staff. Once it was sealed behind a transparent barrier, the CEO bent down and took a good look, against the warnings of numerous highly concerned Admins. It looked like a little skeleton might be cropping up at random places in the stuff just long enough to form a limb and pull itself along before it would collapse, then a new limb appeared somewhere else in the puddle, which was now becoming more of a blob. Bio readings performed by the agents indicated that the player was indeed dead in RL due to some catastrophic interface error, probably as a result of his illegally constructed hardware. Liz had her doubts.

Eleven

Back at his apartment the next morning, Eric was determined to make himself a higher quality breakfast. He paid extra close attention and strived to make it a satisfying extra-large omelet (his dad's favorite) with peppers, onions, mushrooms, and his mother's specialty seasoning. Eric carried his plate over to the dining room table, now completely clutter free for the first time in years. This morning was about investing in life moment to moment from here on out, and getting the most out of life that he could.

Seeing what happened to Ken Faraday jarred Eric. Seeing what happened to Lester, his dramatic death, that jarred him too. All Eric wanted to focus on now were the good things in life, the things that were within his reach, things he could appreciate – good food, good TV, good books, good music. He did have work that night. Another graveyard shift. That didn't bother him in the slightest though. He was ready for a bit more RL in his life.

Working the dough lines later that night, normally this shift would have been what Eric described as a bad night. Gavin was joined by a few new bullies who were eager to have their potshots and get some belly laughs out of the peanut gallery. Eric wouldn't let them get his goat. He promised himself he wouldn't.

"Man, you got the face of a weasel don't you?" One of the newbies sneered.

"What's wrong with your chin? Looks like a little nub or something." Gavin earned some chuckles and a few elbows from

139

his buddies.

Eric didn't look at them. He was focusing on the book he'd brought to the breakroom. He was managing to keep his promise to himself, for now, but the dramatic scene that had unfolded with Lester still echoed in his thoughts.

"Bet that little nub of a jaw would break right off if I slugged him one," taunted Gavin, who put every facial muscle he had into coming off as threatening, but Eric didn't even turn his head. Gavin stormed off, powerless and defeated, without the reward that he was used to getting from Eric so easily.

It was going to be a good day, Eric decided. He didn't have any problem with making sure the machines worked properly during his shift, and he hardly noticed the minutes tick by.

There was only a faint murmur of someone checking out books and the click-clacking of keyboards when Candy started her day's work at the library that afternoon. She loved books. They were right up there with videogames on her list of favorite things. Similarly to Eric, Candy (that is, Robyn) had been shaken by what had happened on the Server, only in her case it was disrupting her concentration.

Time passed.

After a while, the elderly woman in front of Robyn had to raise her thin, reedy voice to get her attention, using the name clearly indicated on her employee badge. Robyn roused from her trance and glanced at the woman. Her face was as worn by the years as the bark of a strong old oak. Six hardcover books lay before her. Evidently she wished to check them all out at the same time. Only these weren't small books. Two looked especially hefty, like they could double as doorstoppers. The thin old woman clearly wasn't going to be able to carry them. Another librarian walked over to promptly explain the matter, saying, "I carried them up here like she asked, but…"

"That's all right, Shannon. I'll handle it." Candy turned an intrigued, sympathetic eye to the woman. If there were a solution to her problem, Candy would have granted it in an instant. There was the delivery service. Of course that would have seemed like the obvious answer, only it wasn't. Candy felt pity and a touch of sorrow for this elder of hers, who wanted only to do something that she probably used to do all the time, something that now had become too difficult as a matter of course, an inevitable end faced by anyone who lived to be as old.

Then, as if she could read Robyn's mind, the woman spoke, "I carried ten books at a time when I was younger. One or two's the most I can do these days. I've heard you offer a home delivery service…"

A muffled din of random chatter distracted Robyn. She struggled to regain her train of thought. A small group of young people accompanied by parents had just arrived and were passing through the turnstile. They were all much younger than the woman at the desk. One of the dads looked like he could probably carry twenty books.

"Yes, we do. We can have all of these books delivered straight to your door. I'll just need to put in an order. What is your name?"

Sam's identity had been under a microscope for the better part of a lifetime, and xe figured this was why it had eventually become so easy to accept this identity of xyrs while loving the skin xe was in. When people are constantly picking you apart, you can either learn to resent yourself or you can do the opposite. That transformation hadn't been immediate. Xe had spent hours, days in xyr room, unwilling, yes, but at times xe'd even been unable to face the day when it was sure to be filled with taunting by friend and family alike. *It is the dilemma of the unpopular,* xe wrote once in xyr journal, *to strive towards meaning without validation. The nonconformist is destined to suffer until xe can accept the condition of xyr reality.*

It had never been of any interest to Sam whether xyr wealthy parents would leave their estate to xem, their offspring. Still, it had always been a bargaining tool that they had used to try to get into xyr head, to get xem to reconsider xyr "life choices", as they put it, in terms of xyr sexual preference (or indeed lack thereof) and xyr non-binary identity. This had always been to Sam the worst of affronts, because if it wasn't bad enough that xyr parents refused to accept xem, they had to dump buckets of salt on the sores by trying to manipulate xem.

No matter. Sam would rise above, create a new name, be someone who was self-determined. Sam's identity had always been an inconvenience to xyr parents, not only because xe didn't want to have a family, which to them, being of the old school, was an unforgivable nightmare, but because image was everything. As well-known and well-liked socialites, they had their demands, and after all, what were they supposed to do – admit defeat and let their child walk all over hundreds of years of tradition? This was their attitude.

Due to a long list of medical issues, they had only been able to bear Sam, and could have no other children, thus aggravating the situation for them. It was also for this reason that they could not relate in the slightest to someone who did not want to have as many children as possible. Threatening to withhold Sam's inheritance had been their last attempt at victory, but Sam would not be conquered. Xe called their bluff and invited their threat, no longer bothering to defend xemself with words. Xyr parent had had decades to change their ways, and it could not have been any clearer to Sam who they really were. No money or supposed love could take away who Sam identified as, and that fact had become a self-reinforcing source of power that kept xem sure of xemself, even when faced with the dimmest regard of which human beings were capable.

"Oh, we're managing darling. Our health endures, but what is good health without new life for the future?"

Sam's mother was honest – some would say too honest. Some would just call it bitchiness. Sam didn't call it anything. It was xyr mother's way, plain and simple.

"How was Thailand?" Sam asked with a smile. "I really liked those pictures you posted."

Sam's father stirred slightly in his lazy boy, trying to get more comfortable. He kept on watching the television and didn't bother joining the conversation.

"The resort was marvelous darling, and the beaches were exquisite. You would have loved it." Xyr mother stared off at her antique crystal lamp, "It would have been a nice beach to walk with a grandchild on."

A wound that felt like it was a billion miles away twinged, but Sam had learned to ignore this through muscle memory. Xe had fought with xyr parents enough times, and making conversation difficult was just their way of coping and avoiding more fights. No, they couldn't let the topic go in its entirety, because they were too obsessed with it, but indirect criticisms were a little easier to ignore than direct ones, Sam figured. Still, it was awkward trying to keep xyr mother from getting a rise out of xem every time xe visited. Always it was forced conversation when there should have been lively exchanges and a thrill for the present, the gift of their time together. But no. Instead, xyr father didn't even look at xem, and xyr mother's voice was soaked with disdain, like always.

"The way you guys rearranged the sunroom looks great."

Xyr mother didn't reply, but gave a semi-happy, partly sad smile. Sam's father didn't move a muscle. Sam pressed on, "The snake plants are a nice addition."

"Yes, well, they're only plants, dear."

Sam nodded, acquiescing xyr mother's tone, dismissive though it was, accepting the tragedy that xe should live in a world where not wanting to have sex was punishable by familial disownment.

They never mentioned their threat of disinheritance any more, not for years. They didn't have to. Their resentment could be heard in every syllable, but Sam loved them still. Xe couldn't simply stop caring for xyr parents who had raised xem through childhood.

In the days before xyr great change and epiphany of identity, Sam had shared a golden era with xyr parents, complete with all the lovely moments you'd expect – learning to ride bicycle, picnics, rolling laughter, games of tag and duck-duck-goose, all the most wonderful things that, at least in memory, could not be destroyed by the complexities of human sexuality and maturity. Xe would be lying to xemself if xe said xe hadn't wished to return to those days, back when xyr parents' eyes would light up with excitement, love, and wonder to see their child playing beneath the sunshine.

Sam wasn't a child any more though. Xe wasn't a woman either, or a man, and people's desire to label xem contrary to xyr wishes felt exactly like the abuse that it was. The whole concept pissed xem off. Why did xe have to say xe was anything in particular, especially in the free world where you could supposedly be whatever you wanted to be?

"I was thinking we could go to the park and have a picnic for Dad's birthday this year like we used to. We could bring a coffee dispenser too. I know you and Dad like a full thermos after lunch."

Still no response from xyr father. Sam's mother deigned to reply, "Sam, really. You don't have to keep doing this."

"Doing what?"

"Coming here like this, stirring things up. It isn't good for your father's heart."

"What are you talking about? I'm just trying to make conversation. What are we supposed to do when I come to visit? Sit around and do nothing?"

Sam's mother was weary by the look on her face, one that of course had taken on wrinkles over the years, but it had taken on something else as well. Or maybe it was something it had lost. Time wasn't to blame, Sam knew that much.

"We just…" xyr mother began. She attempted to sound civil anyway. "We just aren't going to change our minds. You are still disinherited."

Sam felt like xe was going to explode.

The topic hadn't been mentioned by any of the three for years. Sam personally hadn't brought it up ever in xyr life because it was never a topic of concern to xem. Xyr parents once had the habit of bringing it up every year or so to try to spur Sam into action.

Sam's first reaction was what you'd expect – xe wanted to defend xemself, fight to clarify xyr reason for wanting to be a part of their lives, as if that wasn't clear as day. That part of xem wanted to forgive them for being so clueless, wanted to blame their vast fortune for poisoning their minds and making them so paranoid and controlling, but the will just wasn't in xem any more. Trying to inspire their attitudes had lost its appeal. Xe sat in silence for a while until xyr mother returned her gaze to the television, and together, her and her husband resumed a reluctant tolerance of their daughter's presence.

Sam crept away unannounced some time later and called for a public Otto. It was late, so xe didn't have to hide xyr sobs from anyone while xe waited at the roundabout in front of the building's entryway.

When xyr Otto arrived and xe got in, Sam opened xyr phone app and put in an order to drive to a random spot across the city. Xe watched the streetlights pass overhead, a classic practice some hundreds of years old, and let xyr thoughts dwindle under the hypnotic effect. Xe later updated xyr order to change direction and go to the other side of the city. Over and over xe did this, spending a whole day's wages in rides around the city before xe was through. It was the motion, xe decided eventually when xe got out of the car after arriving back at xyr low-income home. While in motion, reality didn't have to be fixed. *Don't let no one slow you down,* xe told xemself. So long as xe kept moving, xe wasn't trapped.

Maxx didn't have a lot of laundry to do. He lived alone. Half of the clothes he had to wash were workout clothes. He had always wanted to have one of those encounters like from the old movies where boy meets boy at a laundromat and the two hit it off. Cue sitcom.

No such luck though. He'd tried hitting on all kinds of cute dudes, and the result was always the same. Romance clearly wasn't a hit at the laundromat. It was like the opposite of a nightclub. Instead of dressing up, flaunting their stuff and throwing themselves into the lap of some hot stranger, people wore scrubby outfits and kept to themselves. Maybe, just maybe they would nod or smile at each other.

The whole scene was unbearable, Maxx thought. Even in thick crowds, he felt a million miles away from the rest of humanity. Every day after his dad passed from the world, Maxx found it harder to want to stick around, and found himself yearning to follow in the ghostly footsteps of his old man. He would scold himself to chase these thoughts away, but it was no use. No relationship felt it could ever be as meaningful as the only relationship that really seemed to matter. Could he ever live up to his father's legacy? No. He couldn't ever fill the shoes of that great man. But he could try.

A nearly hairless blue-eyed lad in his twenties tried to strike up a conversation with Maxx. His train of thought derailed, Maxx found himself unable to react. He was stuck in wallowing mode and ended up ignoring the cute boy, *THE* cute boy that could have been Mr. Right, once again, and this time it would haunt him for weeks.

Of course, every Tom, Dick, and Harry has to be here with their mother and movie cast entourage tonight, Liz seethed. *People everywhere.* All she wanted to do was get the groceries she needed for the week and get home. Grocery deliveries had been discontinued in her neighborhood temporarily due to wage-related labor strikes.

Liz supported the cause of the Otto mechanics one hundred percent, but it took everything she had to face the crowds on this night. The face and pathological mission of that man whose name she now feared to say, whose avatar she feared to name, lingered

147

in her perception of everything around her. If such a man could sprout and take root among the males of her own backyard, how could she trust a single one of them? She couldn't, she decided. It's not like she hadn't always been sure of that, but it was a glaring issue now, one she struggled to tolerate with every breath. Men came within inches of her, doing nothing more than grabbing some peanut butter or an avocado, and her flesh crawled.

This isn't forever, Liz, she told herself. *You're going to get through this, you're going to get back home and you'll finally be alone. No games for a while.* She would lock the doors and windows, then triple check the locks later that night. She would leave her books on the shelves, leave the television off along with all her other devices. She would paint, listen to instrumental music, and sing. She would soak up the sweet absence of other people and dive into a pile of abstraction.

Nameless forms would take the place of words, words which to her would have been meaningless during this time spent cut off from the others. Brushstrokes and lilting vocalizations were her frustrated screams and tears. It was her habit every now and then to unplug from the grid for a while and eat peanut butter with avocadoes, except tonight she flashed back to the grocery store and broke down all over again. Faces and bodies by the thousands. A stampede in the making should the worst happen. The worst? A mass shooting. Thoughts of worst-case scenarios haunted her until she sang away the pain and melted back into another painting, another composition.

Twelve

The long isolation was over. A week-long hiatus from gadgetry might have been a walk in the park for some, but to Liz an age had gone by. *Baby steps,* she decided on the morning that she logged back into the Virtua Server after a masterfully gourmet round of avocado toast and ants on a log. Prium was the kind of place that would have been her last choice during her hiatus, but there was one area she knew would only be sparsely populated with human players, if at all. The back alleys that hid the city's thieves guilds were full of spaces that were vacant or nearly empty. A perfect place to start.

Upon opening her eyes in Dagthrim Alley, Liz found only NPCs waiting there beside scattered vendor windows. The characters occupied a universe that was somewhere between *Cyberpunk 2077* and *Charles Dickens*. They were hunched over, some even huddled next to low-burning barrels.

Liz took her time. The whole point was not to rush, so she traced the edges of every surface, examined the ground, the varying quality of the pavement, the patches of exposed brick and dripping pipes. Gritty sounds of puddles, the rain, and unalive AI chatter echoed through the alleys as Liz made her way down one path, then another. She had no idea where she was going, which was the whole point. The nooks and crannies of this quiet place unfolded before her like promising little secrets waiting to be discovered. There was something that was inexplicably beautiful about the ordinary in that moment. The gently varying patterns of brickwork in building facades and in walkways, the blurred graphics where the hard lines of reality would have met.

Something caught her eye just then. Was she being followed? Whatever it was, she saw in her peripheral vision that it had darted behind a vendor's tent. *Should I scour the alley?* She realized that she must have been imaging things when she walked around the tent and found nothing.

"Would you look at this place," Agent Marcus urged his coworkers who were still cleaning up the Tanzen Plaza. A whole week later, and both this area and the random rock wall outside Prium were still off-limits to players while company staff studied and repaired the affected infrastructure. "That fiasco could have put the Server out of commission for months. Good thing Ash showed up when she did."

Marcus and his team's orders were to scan, rescan, and scan some more. Most of the days consisted of rechecking their work. They were finally getting to the end of the process. Now was the time to patch up the last remaining wounds in the programming.

"You know, they said that one incel hacker died in the attack." Agent Shawn shifted into a tone of macabre humor. "His love life killed his love for life."

"I heard that was all based on some signal readings that could have been faked," offered Agent Missy, who spoke while she worked. "The guy had a lot of motive for wanting to make a clean getaway. He would have been facing some serious time for the hacking and kidnapping alone, not to mention the rest of his plan, which the company claims to be aware of but has refused to release any information. Did they ever get the hacker's name?"

"It was mentioned, but I don't remember it," replied Marcus.

"Me neither," the other two followed.

"I still remember the avatar name though. *Runsdeep* something or other. It had a number too, like 999 or something, but the name was Runsdeep. Kind of a weird name, right?" asked Missy.

"Yeah, well he was a weird dude," Shawn chortled as he continued sweeping his scans this way and that. "If he faked his death or whatever that would be so messed up. There are rumors, I'm pretty sure, that the avatar has been seen since the attack. Who knows if that's true though?"

"It's no use wondering whether or not that's possible or the case now, is it?" asked a fourth employee, who had been silent up until now. Over the course of the previous week, Terryl had mostly kept to himself.

The rest of the team halted their scans, and Shawn retorted, "Why not? You never know, man. Anything is possible."

"Yeah, that's the point, isn't it?" Terryl sounded sour. There was an edge to his voice. Everyone heard it. It was almost unmistakable, but they said nothing of the fact that it sounded like Terryl sympathized with the hacker, and probably even felt sad that he had been defeated. This made Missy's skin crawl and Shawn's guts turn.

"Because unless you run into him, you would never have any way of knowing whether he's still out there," Terryl said, still without looking at the others.

Not liking his creepy contribution, the rest of the team dropped the subject, but Terryl chanted to himself like it was his mantra, *somebody on the Server has to know the truth.*

The muscles in Maxx's legs were being pushed to the extreme in today's workout. Swollen, hot and girthy, his real body wasn't nearly as muscular as his videogame avatar, but he definitely looked like the personal trainer he was. Cut abs, formidable thighs, and a dangerous set of arms. He looked like the kind of action man that would have gone toe-to-toe on the big screen with the likes of Sean Claud Van Damme and Sylvester Stallone. Exercise was a perfect object of focus. Nameless. Voiceless. The movements and weights were extensions of Maxx's body interacting with the cosmos. His pecs and shoulders rippled with the dynamic tension that pulled at him. Silent. Interactive. The weights pulled back, mirroring his insistence. One bicep relaxed, the other pulled. The opposite. And again. His breathing carried a mechanical rhythm, a command over his surroundings, an escape from the flesh, or perhaps a running to, a joining in dance, a negotiation with reality. Sweat trickled from his brush-like eyebrows.

Maxx thought about Lester, *Runsdeep,* how there must have been others like him out there, all little ticking time bombs in need of defusing. Who was going to take that job though, be the bomb defusal expert? He pulled harder at the weights, tearing new power into his form, determined to be ready.

Terryl was alone, which wasn't unusual. He spent a lot of time alone, and most of the time it wasn't by choice. People didn't like him. It wasn't that he was unpleasant, he'd been informed. Being a Monitor for Virtua meant that he sometimes had to work with other staff, and they found him tolerable for the most part. Fortunately he never had to talk about anything that wasn't work-related, so he didn't. Not even when people tried to be nice and ask him about his life. He would simply ignore any such attempts at friendliness, because he honestly didn't believe kindness was a real thing. Kindness, in truth and evidence, was nothing more than an animal's attempt to exert influence over another animal's senses, as far as he was concerned. If you were nice to people, they would be nice to you, and maybe help you out if you ever really needed something. The whole charade made him want to puke.

The last remaining nonessential program bug wasn't an emergency by any means, but fixing it was a task Terryl had to complete. He was glad to be assigned a ticket that he could do on his own. Terryl experienced frequent insomnia, and the way he saw it, "If I can get ahead of this work before daybreak, my cuck boss can assign me even more work than he would have otherwise, and, in time, if I bust my ass and work really hard, I can get promoted and get myself a nice trophy wife who'll marry me for the money before turning me into a cuck as well."

The question of *why* didn't really come into Terryl's mind very often, rather *how* – how could he survive another day without jumping off a bridge?

A voice called to him, some disembodied voice that traveled about the room sounding of cold, liquid metal. Terryl froze.

The last bug... you Monitors are crafty, aren't you?

Terryl was fascinated and afraid. How could this be happening? Having exposed the Server architecture to its barest filaments, he knew that no one could be using any kind of cloak without his knowledge. Nobody, that is... could it be?

"It's the last thread, or the last cord of rope. Frazzled, but fixable," Terryl replied.

The strands that bind an entire world together bend at your fingertips. You must crave to do more with such power.

It occurred to Terryl that the voice could be the master hacker himself back from the dead. This was Terryl's lucky day. It had been his dream to join forces with Runsdeep someday. Maybe that's how the hacker found him. And after months of only the

153

briefest chats, the day had finally come. Terryl struggled to contain his excitement and answered, "There is a lot more sophisticated programming to be done, it's true."

That's not what you want to do though, is it?

"If I'm being honest, no. The job has sort of been a way to fill time."

A way to kill time, you mean. How often do you think about it?

"About what?" Terryl scowled.

Killing yourself.

Terryl's scowl hardened. How could the voice have known? After all their conversations, Lester had never spoken to him this way. Still, the only explanation was that it was indeed the master hacker himself, the sultan of suffering, who all this time must have been looking to Terryl and learning about his life. Terryl's time had come.

"...every day," Terryl admitted, tears welling up.

The metallic voice continued, *You simply crave the life you were meant to live. The life of a man. I can help you do something about that. I can't promise you women, but I can promise you a cause. In my experience, the cause is all anyone like us needs to survive until tomorrow.*

Terryl was hooked.

"Tell me more," he urged.

The disembodied voice chuckled on, *I have a plan that is already in motion, but it cannot be fulfilled without you.*

Candy's home was not a lonely place. Far from it. She had been happily wed to the love of her life on a sunny Bali beach in 2048, after which domestic bliss ensued. Paula was the wife of her dreams, and Candy reminded her of it every day. What so many would perceive as a perfect relationship was not enough to quell her body image issues, however.

Body dysmorphic disorder had been the topic of therapy sessions and medicinal treatment, and with plenty of support from her wife, Candy got by. Paula rubbed her shoulders that evening with cucumber melon lotion. Paula could tell that she was tense. She couldn't stand to see her that way, so she set to working that masseuse magic that Candy, or rather Robyn, was so enthralled by.

"Quit looking at yourself like that in the mirror, please," Paula gently requested. Robyn defiantly refused, her eyes obsessed with her love handles, love handles that got all the use a woman could ever want in a sex life.

"Like what? I mean it, have I gained weight?"

Paula's warm hands left Robyn's skin wanting and scized the mirror by its sides, flipping it around so that it faced the wall instead. Robyn pouted playfully.

Paula asked, "You're not going to play your videogame tonight, are you?"

"It's time I got back to my bitches."

"Ah yes," Paula heard the endearing term often, "bitches are important. Just don't forget your main bitch is dying to try your soufflé tonight."

They kissed long and hard, briefly interrupting their usual, more delicate interaction. Giving Candy's chin a quick caress before retreating back to the downstairs floor of their comfortable apartment, Paula was off for her second workout of the day. She didn't really play videogames. Only on rare occasions when Candy asked her to. She was an athlete and a city lawyer, so motivation was not an issue for her, whereas Candy was motivated mainly as a housewife.

155

Leading a sedentary life, Candy, which is the fantasy name Robyn chose for herself after one of her favorite things in the world, wanted to start doing something about her weight, and she was determined to be proactive this time. She didn't have to get ripped abs like Paula or be able to run five miles a day. No, she wanted it because Paula was concerned for her health, because their doctor was concerned.

The couple had discussed Paula's day at the firm earlier on. Candy recalled this for a moment and looked at the selfie she had taken with her wife and her artistic photo of the new wine glasses they picked up from Goodwill. She recalled sophisticated conversation of the kind Paula was so well known for over a platter of cranberry crostini that Candy had prepared. Paula had expressed a willingness to try a little more fantasy, maybe read some fiction for a change. A lightbulb went on in Candy's head.

"Honey!" Candy called.

Paula pulled back, halfway out the door, "What?"

"Will you come back up here for a second, please?"

Terryl had been waiting for around half an hour in the basement of a random building in an MMO shooter subserver when Lester's metallic voice gurgled to him again. Just as before, his voice floated around as though it were part of a gust of wind, never staying in one place.

Did you bring everything I asked for?

"Yeah. Coding applicator and the specific Darwin source codes. It's all right here," Terryl replied and indicated his inventory to the voice. The voice degenerated into a melodic scraping that squealed and whined in something like an emotional response.

Do exactly as I ask. Point the applicator to the southern wall and engage Darwin code 4-alpha-might/co.setframe.

Terryl did as requested and was instantly struck with an outward flow of dark silver particles that burst from the wall and coalesced around his applicator and arm. The particles formed a black, reflective layer of liquid metal that dimly mirrored the surroundings. The black ooze slithered around his body, acquainting itself with him before flowing deep into his head like water down a drain. The voice no longer spoke from the room, but from within Terryl's skull. It told him he had work to do and that all would become clear in time.

"So you really think this is going to be a good workout for me?" Paula asked.

Of course she's skeptical, Candy thought. What Paula considered to be thorough exercise would have been boot camp to Candy.

"I'm really glad I got a two-person track system so that we can at least give this a try together," Candy said. "Most of the game happens in your head, but you do jump, roll, and run in RL while you play, so yeah, it should be a workout as long as we get you moving!"

"RL?" Paula asked. Candy forgot that, as one who tended toward all things non-fiction, Paula didn't know the vocabulary of the virtual world. Candy smirked, to the slight irritation of Paula, who further asked, "Are you going to tell me or just make fun of me?"

"It's not that. It's just that you're a videogame virgin, sort of."

"Yeah, pretty much. I played them a couple times when I was a kid." Paula thought back to that summer when her best friends were two sandy-haired boys who liked video games and kicking up rocks on dirt roads with their go-carts.

Candy and Paula changed into more comfortable clothes that would allow for full range of motion. When they were all set and each stood on their own side of the track system, Candy checked in with her partner one last time before the two donned their VirtuaHelms.

"You sure you want to do this? It might be a letdown."

"Not if I'm with you," Paula said with a sigh, reaching to hold Candy's hand. They looked into each other's knowing, loving gazes, pulled the VR headsets down over their eyes, and were sped away to the Server.

Thirteen

Hours had passed by the time Sam's Otto finally arrived at the hole in the wall where xe lived above a bar that hosted live bands. Xyr parents had of course been appalled at xyr choice of living conditions, but this only made xem like the place even more. *Live to like the rough life* was xyr secret mantra.

The ceiling had three steady leaks (*Or was it four?* Sam wondered) for which xe owned as many buckets, and there wasn't one spot in the whole place where the floor didn't creak. At least whenever xe needed fresh air all xe had to do was stand by the one window where there was a strong draft. Every time xyr parents saw the place they offered to put xem up in a fancy suite somewhere with a ceiling twenty feet high. Sam politely refused every single time, knowing that the offer wasn't open-ended. Xyr parents had never accepted xem. *Never will,* xe said to xemself.

Once inside xyr apartment with the door locked, Sam made xyr rounds to all xyr little pets. A fish tank as big as a pool table held center stage in xyr living room. An automatic timer would release fish food as needed. The tank had its roof modified with cardboard to protect from ceiling leaks.

Sam would always make a point to linger by each of the four glass sides and talk to xyr fish. Companions. Community fish. Although these little life forms, like xem, had only short lives to live, xyr little aquatic pets didn't have to defend themselves against a hostile world. Sam took care of all that. It made xem

159

feel powerful in a way, like xe was in control.

After depositing two heaping clumps of mashed fruit into xyr gecko tank and sprinkling a few crickets into xyr tarantula tank, Sam retired to the couch where xe wrapped xemself up and scrolled through social media. Xyr father was ranting about corrupt politicians again. Even though xe couldn't stand the things that he would say and post, Sam didn't have the heart to unfollow, remove, or block xyr father's account. He wouldn't talk to her in person, so these were the only words of his that xe got to experience any more. Part of xem yearned to go against all logic and share his post or leave a supportive comment just to have some kind of exchange with him once again. Then the sound of the downstairs door buzzer roused xem from that line of thinking.

Jan and Sam had met in art school and always made a point to see each other for coffee at least once a month. It was hard to come up with conversation some days, but not today.

"Can you believe that hacker was never found? They tried to triangulate his broadcasting location, but it was a cold case. He could still be at large!" Jan sounded more impressed than afraid.

"So much for a light chat," Sam blew at xyr fresh cup to cool it off.

"Oh, and there are loads of conspiracy theories already too. I had one streaming on my way over here. That Cho guy. Anyway, he thinks there's a wannabe masquerading as the hacker, recruiting incels for something they call The Cause. Other people think Lester faked his death and planned the whole encounter to lull everyone into a false sense of security."

"But wait, why would he whip up security twice if he wanted to sow a false sense of security?" Sam didn't buy it.

"He couldn't help it. He's a genius. Showing off is like

breathing to him, and in the meantime – you just watch – he'll strike again. Who knows how, who knows when!"

"You've been watching too much TV."

"You might be right about that," Jan admitted and drew a long sip of her own cup. She loved her mysteries and police procedurals. RL though? It had another level of unpredictability. Nobody was worried about ratings in RL, at least not in the same way, which made it all the more exciting.

She started to go on about a TV series that the whole hacker crisis reminded her of when Sam cut her off frantically, "This can't be possible!" Sam's breath was gone, taken away.

"What is it? What's happening? Did they find him?" Jan, again, seemed more curious than concerned. Sam flipped xyr tablet around to show Jan the headline, and she gasped.

Logging on was the easy part. It was like waking up from a deep sleep or from a dream. Having only seen screenshots of Candy's albino ferret avatar before this moment, and being fully aware of Candy's bully-induced, self-conscious reason for using it, Paula complimented Candy, "You look so cuddly! Almost as cuddly as your real body," then she yowled like a cat. Candy assumed a curtsied modelling pose and blew Paula a kiss.

Taking the lead with a light jog, determined to make good on her promise of exercise, Candy led Paula through that place called Prium, where historic Las Vegas neon signs meet *Tron,* meets Rainbow Road on *Super Mario Cart.* In that way it was exactly what Paula had been expecting – like being in a planet-sized arcade, and Candy knew that the subserver she had in mind was going to be a real surprise.

Veering into an urban park and jogging under a neat mason archway, Paula gasped to see the grassy park suddenly stretch out in all directions, as though the city had been grabbed by some massive computer cursive somewhere, clicked, and dragged away at a million miles an hour. When the land finally stopped moving and stretching, she was surrounded by rainforest. A rushing stream ran alongside her and Candy. It wasn't as good as real life, but it approached a level of real that fooled the mind into believing that it was good enough, especially with the smells of petrichor and reflections in the water.

It occurred to Paula how this place could be miraculous to someone who was paralyzed or mobility impaired. The smells combined with the tiniest sensations, like grains of dirt and the feel of breeze, had the potential to let anyone travel the globe and beyond without even leaving their bed. Use of the VirtuaHelm™ track system had been meant to make the game even more immersive, but in the future it would not be required (perhaps in the very near future, what with Lester's technology having been discovered). The company had long been running outreach campaigns that showed off this potential to the whole world, but Paula had been too consumed by her work to even notice.

She and Candy chased each other around the trees for a while. It was a rush! Like joining your best friend in a dream world. A boundless energy filled them.

Paula took full advantage of the momentum by talking to the first people they ran into, "Hello! How are you? Today's my first day here!" Paula was giddy as a schoolgirl with a teddy for show and tell.

"Hi…" replied one of the young ladies, who was obviously too cool to mirror Paula's enthusiasm. Her friends said nothing. Their underwhelming response didn't slow Paula down.

"Where to next? What's over here?" Candy, who didn't have time to answer because Paula was already on the move, mumbled a sorry to the ladies mixed with a good-bye and followed.

The forest opened into a tranquil field. Not far away they saw a series of large tents pitched where people played music and danced. It was a Renaissance Faire subserver!

Pleased with the unexpected turn of events, Paula dove straight into the concentric circles of dancing people, making it up as she went along. Candy observed and had a big belly laugh. They moved on eventually to peruse the vendors and sample the fire-roasted dainties. Never actually eating, diners did experience an incredible sensation of "almost-eating", experiencing both flavor and the sensation of food entering the belly. Masse cultural revolution was on the horizon, Virtua had forewarned. The question remained as to what the world was going to look like after the revolution.

"Care to test your wit, milady?" A thin, sparkly-eyed fellow asked, bowing and hamming it up. Paula was up for anything.

"Why, yes, good sir, I believe I do!" Without delay, the man led the two past a great long line of tents that were selling a cornucopia of wares, mostly food, clothes, trinkets and games, keeping a lowered, Quasimodo-type stance as he hurried along. Some fifty paces beyond the last tent there was one of a much different style than the rest. It tickled the curiosity. Exchanging a mutually quick and affirmative glance, Candy and Paula pressed on, led by the thin man.

"What is your name, good sir?"

"Terryl, milady. And yours?"

"It's…" *Play pretend,* Paula told herself, "Priscilla and Candice." Candy squinted a smile at her. *Roleplaying – how fun,* Candy thought! This Terryl guy was sure to be a treat. Candy figured he had some kind of crystal ball inside this mysterious, shoddy-looking tent, along with a few puzzle games, or tarot cards, or–

"Come, come inside," the man insisted as he ducked and disappeared beneath the thick drapes that covered the entrance.

Paula hesitated, turned to Candy and asked, "This is fine, right? I mean, we can't get hurt here or nothing, and we can take the helmets off whenever we want, right?"

Candy knew that this was the case, but something still didn't feel right. What if he was a total creep? Why have his tent so far from the others?

"Maybe we should turn back–"

The man poked his head out from under the drapes,

"Come, come!"

Paula shrugged and went inside. Candy hesitated, then followed. The inside was cleaner and more organized than expected. No crystal ball, no mini games. There wasn't much at all besides one chair, a table (both out of place in their mundane style), and a small, gray box. There was nothing about the box that made it seem important besides the fact that it was the only thing of any relevance in the room. Why was it there? Paula immediately took it as a puzzle. Terryl stood motionless as the two women took in their surroundings, then he picked up the gray box.

"Life is a puzzle, isn't it?"

Terryl eyed the box vacantly. This made Paula uneasy.

"Is this a riddle?" She was goal-oriented as ever.

"No," Terryl replied, then fell silent for a moment, testing Paula's patience before he finished the thought. "This is the answer."

A black ooze surged from the box and coated Terryl's body. Recognizing the horrible stuff in an instant, Candy desperately searched for the drapes to exit the tent, but they had disappeared.

She screamed, and her scream fueled the ooze. It pulsed and changed color, returning to the same, glistening black with alternating beats. The surface of the ooze bubbled out long welts and swelled, taking on the appearance of muscle as it quivered and grew. Terryl's face was overtaken by the ooze last, and the whole monstrosity pulsed red and purple, with tiny bursts of white in between that made the room glow. Back to glistening black, the monstrous man's hand shot out and gripped Paula's arm, and the ooze began to spread.

Candy fell to the ground terrified before she could gather her wits, then charged the foe. Without unhanding her partner, Terryl pivoted on the ball of one foot and swept the other in a furious kick, booting Candy clear from the tent and straight out of the subserver, landing in front of the archway portal at the entrance to the park.

It was the middle of the day, and it wasn't a work day, which meant Eric could hang out. He'd already gotten his family visit in for the week (Mom and Dad wanted to hear all about the cool new videogame system), so now he could really soak up the chill time without feeling like he was slacking off. There wouldn't be much on the agenda. Maybe he'd listen to a little music, do a little doodling, clean up the garbage that littered his apartment. He'd always wanted to learn French.

Eric let his thoughts wander, shouldering absent-mindedly the lessons he'd learned in the last week. He'd been at one of his lowest points ever, he realized. *Up and out of this ditch,* he reckoned. Meeting Lester had taught him that there were other people who struggled similarly to the way he had.

More at peace now with his experience of life, and more interested in the potential of each moment and whatever the future might bring, Eric wasn't ashamed any more, partly because he'd met people whose own relationships with sex were unique to him. And yet, the LGBTQIA+ friends he'd made, Liz and her crew, to him they seemed like misfits or rebels. And they weren't just another group of people, Eric decided. They were people who in different ways meant something to him now. Friends who, to a certain degree, he loved. *How fortunate to have friends in life,* he thought.

An incessant, rapid beeping triggered his annoyed response – a frustrated growl – and he rose to look at his phone. It was an emergency message from Liz. It read, *GET YOUR ASS ONLINE RIGHT NOW WE HAVE A SITUATION.*

Candy rocked in her seat, barely containing her sobs. She had logged out to check on Paula only to find her catatonic, and removing the helmet had put her into a never-ending, incurable seizure. Horrified, Candy returned the helmet to her dear wife's head, which stopped the seizing, but still didn't bring her round from wherever the monster Terryl had taken her.

Emergency staff were contacted. Private doctors were dispatched to Candy's residence but were unable to determine a solution and promptly left. To the whole squad's surprise, Virtua kept the Server up and running. No news was to be shared about the incident, and Candy and her friends were urged to not say a word until their rapid-response teams could track Paula down. Secrecy was paramount to success, they said. Candy couldn't help but wonder if they were full of shit.

Liz was possessed. She would not rest until Paula was safely back in Candy's loving arms. Sam was quiet, though clearly disturbed. Maxx held Candy stoically as she sobbed, acting as her steady rock. They all thought they had been through the worst together, but this? What were they supposed to do? Their answer would come in the form of an Admin, who flashed into existence with a puff of smoke, graceful as a ballerina.

"Come with me," ordered the Admin.

United States President Yessica Li Lundgrasse and Virtua CEO Ashley Quinn Fournier convened at one end of a round table, the kind you'd see at the UNE (United Nations of Earth). A hundred experts, scientists, and corporate lawyers were there with them, along with a host of Admins. Eric, Liz and the squad had been seated alongside the CEO for some reason. Ashley spoke with an air of self-assured confidence even in this time, and it made Candy want to punch her.

"Look, people, we are going to watch this video, as you insist that we must, but I have to stress that our own conflict resolution staff is more than prepared to handle the current situation."

President Lundgrasse, dressed in her best suit and poised to knock Ashley from her perch, retorted, "All respect to your teams, Ms. Fournier, but the ship of conflict resolution sailed a long time ago. This is, what, the third time you've experienced catastrophic hacking? Do you really think congress will let this technology of yours live to see the end of the month? If you don't take this seriously and listen to my taskforce personnel, that terrorist is going to get away with this, and you're going to pay the price."

The CEO kept her face perfectly still, not showing a shred of the rage that filled her. Her company was on top of the world. Nobody could change that. Even if they outlawed the technology in the United States, other countries were ready to take her in. Her life as a corporate queen was guaranteed, she told herself, so why get upset? She nodded in acquiescence. One of the president's eyebrows ticked with attitude, and she gave the signal for her staff to start the slideshow, led by a military man in decorated uniform.

"Slide One: we know that the new rogue virus' handle is self-designated as Runsdeep991. That means that the hacker who designed it wanted to be identified, or else it wouldn't bear this digital nametag," the military man traced beneath the name to point it out. "So far, we can't tell if the virus is completely autonomous or if it's being at least partially controlled. What we *can* tell is that it features many of the same automatic subroutines, shared by our NPCs, which are present in the virus' software, so it did likely have a predetermined purpose, a mission to complete. Like an NPC, our theory is that it is driven by a single purpose, one from which it isn't likely to deviate."

Sam had xyr arms crossed. Xe wasn't sure if xe accepted this explanation. It made logical sense that Lester might leave behind a hacked NPC to do his bidding, but Candy had told everyone about the man named Terryl. *Maybe they should come up with a theory about who he is,* Sam thought. The wall projection, which dwarfed the room, displayed the next slide, and the military man went on,

"We believe that this man, known as Terryl Fornelli," he said, tracing a circle around his head in last snapshot taken by System AI before Terryl walked into the tent with Candy and Paula, "must have some affiliation with the hacker."

You think? Sam cursed inside. Who was this guy anyway? Where did he come from? Redundancy was necessary, Sam supposed. Maxx knew that. His dad would have said that *a good car will last you as long as you pay attention to every removable part.*

168

"Terryl was, until about ten minutes ago, a Virtua employee who worked as a Monitor. This is potentially your biggest problem," Mr. Military looked at Ashley Fournier gravely, "because if Virtua employees can be so swiftly recruited by this man, or his virus, or however he's doing it…" Mr. Military was becoming visibly frustrated. It was clear that this was a new type of enemy to him, on a new type of battlefield.

President Lundgrasse remained on her feet, stood tall, and addressed Ash, "You don't even know what he could have wanted with that poor woman," she declared. *Her name is Paula,* Candy screamed inside. "If you don't solve this and find her in twenty-four hours, we're pulling the plug. You can't be allowed to endanger more human lives."

"You're not pulling anything without congress," Ashley Fournier shot back confidently. "Try, and I'll have the whole thing tied up in the courts for years. It'll become center stage for your presidency and will define your memory in history. You're playing with the big girls now, princess."

The president lost all composure and lunged across the round table. Staff and secret service streamed after, trying to stop her, but she found her target all the more quickly, tackling the CEO off her chair and pinning her to the floor with a violent thud. Ashley thrashed and kicked up at Yessica, and when she finally connected with her chest she sent the president four feet off the ground.

Lundgrasse landed on the edge of the round table back-first. The whole horrible scene made Liz cheer inside. Eric, out of instinct and forgetting about the immortality granted by the Server, ducked and ran for cover, worried the secret service would soon start shooting people. With viruses and hackers calling the shots lately, who could say what was impossible now?

"Ladies, ladies, please!" One of the Admins got between the two alphas duking it out after the president recovered and tried to dive for the CEO again. "Is this your solution? Enough! How do you want history to remember you, again?"

The two women were successfully restrained by droves of people with opposing interests, many of whom were starting to get at each other's throats now too. Liz wanted to dash into the middle and taunt both sides, egg them on to a renewed melee, but she contained herself. She didn't actually blame any of them. She just loved seeing people who thought they were in control lose their shit. Maxx on the other hand wanted the exact opposite, and made it so. "Is this the message we're sending the world?" Maxx's face was flushed and hot with anger. This man of imposing, assertive presence was quickly noticed by all, and their clamoring diminished so that they could better hear him. Maxx marched over to the table and occupied the noticeable gap between the opposing interest groups in their suits and ties. He held his hands on his hips, looked everyone over, then resumed his monologue to a now-silent room, "An innocent woman has been kidnapped by sick-minded men whose goal in life is to objectify the global female population," his torso muscles bounced as he flexed for emphasis, "and your answer is to bicker and fight? Don't you understand what's at stake here?"

Maxx turned to Ashley Fournier, "Your technology holds the promise of freeing humankind from the limitations of the body. The medical world, recreation, travel, billions of people will see their lives changed. A person can now pilot a robot from anywhere on the planet in real time, meaning anyone anywhere could potentially work from home. What was it you said on Unicorn Riot's livestream last month? That the Virtua Server was going to be the safest place in the world? That with robots and the VirtuaHelm^{TM}, no one would ever be tempted to risk their life to make a good living ever again?"

The CEO looked away with a hint of shame. The Server hadn't turned out to be so safe after all, at least not for the time being.

"And you!" Maxx directed his ferocity at President Lundgrasse. "Leader of the free world loses patience and launches an unprovoked attack. Could you be any more of an embarrassment?"

He buried his face in his palms for a second, then went on. "A degree of finesse is called for, don't you see? A surgical knife rather, not a samurai sword. This battle, real as any battle you face in the world today, Ms. President, can't be won without swallowing our pride and accepting each other's help. You've got anti-cyberhacker teams by the truckload, I'm sure. Get them to team up with us and Fournier's people. We'll bring the dream back to life."

President Lundgrasse looked the same as everyone else – eyes wide, forehead tense. Her words betrayed this look of composure, "Can any of you tell me who the hell this guy is?"

"I'm with them," Maxx pointed over at the squad, who straightened themselves up best as they could when the president and CEO's eyes fell on them. New friends and old, they held a piece of the puzzle that the power duo would need if they were going to save the promise that Virtua's technology held for their country and for the world. Their mutual enemy had a face and a name, but their cause would reach well beyond this one man and the range of his influence. It was about keeping people like him from ever terrorizing the Server again. The squad offered ideas of their own and exchanged information with the company and the US government officials in attendance. The prior chaos was supplanted with the calm of reason. The Admins insisted every subserver be scanned.

"We'll sweep every corner, every crack, every blade of grass," Admin One declared with a booming voice as though he were dropping the mic at the end of a debate. Such scanning wouldn't be necessary, however.

The news wasn't announced. It simply appeared on the wall projector. Eric didn't see who switched it to Gamersage31's livestream, but he did notice immediately that there were over three hundred thousand viewers. The audience had been captivated by what they saw unfolding high above the hub city of Prium. Surreal glitches shot out of a swirling mist like the stray tentacles of a barely contained sea monster, lashing out in the manner of whipcracks.

The Server's automatic defenses were quickly acting to contain the bizarre threat, yet the mass was growing. Only slightly but growing all the same. There floated at the center of the fog a humanoid figure. Ash ordered her nearest employee to zoom in on the figure, and the Admin rushed to do so, pushing Eric and Liz out of her way. As the camera panned in, everyone could see that the fog was actually a rushing disturbance of pixels similar to the texture that wind gives to water in RL. At the center of the rotating disturbance floated the virus. Dark, branch-like filaments stretched out from its body like omnidirectional roots that were sucking at the essence of the Server. Somehow sensing whose eyes were now upon it, the avatar snapped its head up to face the camera.

Candy hopped up onto the round table and loaded her rocket launcher. President Lundgrasse instinctively ducked down behind her security personnel. Candy stared at the screen, eyes locked with the ooze-covered face of the virus. In its arms rested the body of Paula, unconscious and helpless. Candy nodded at the CEO, saying, "Time to whine or shine, ma'am."

Fourteen

The arca surrounding the Runsdeep monstrosity was raging now. Encroaching waves of glitching graphics peeled away at the textural layers of Prium's tallest buildings and were beginning to erode their structural elements as well. Paula remained unconscious. Candy could see as much when she peered through the zoom feature of her own fancy new avatar. Moments earlier Ash tapped each member of the squad on the shoulder, and sparkly clouds wrapped around them and solidified into *Gundam-style* armor. Liz had exclaimed, "Badass!"

The new avatars and the powers they imbued boosted the crew's confidence, but they were still afraid. The creature or whatever it was made everyone nervous with its unsettling posture. It moved its head in constant jerks like an insect or a bird. Candy howled in frustration, causing everyone to flinch. Eric and Maxx, who stood closest to her, tried to quiet her, but she only howled louder. Paula began to rouse from her slumber, "…Robyn?"

"It's me! We're here for you! Don't be afraid, honey!"

CEO Ashley Quinn Fournier hesitated when she saw the virus drop its arms and the first moments of Paula's rapid descent. Candy on the other hand screamed and bolted for her, lifting off from the ground as her god-mode suit naturally responded to her pressing need to save her wife. Ash thought about the woman lying in an apartment somewhere in LA, her mind imprisoned within the construct of her videogame system. A viral infiltration run amok, true, but it was still all on her as leader of the company. *I've created a monster, haven't I?* She wrestled with the question. Candy caught Paula before her body could collide with the pitiless dirt, then doubled back to the group with her wife firmly clutched to her furry chest. President Lundgrasse floated up alongside her, flanked by her security detail. Technically the president was breaking the law by putting herself in such danger by so much as even stepping foot, so to speak, inside the Server at a time when viruses were hijacking people's brains, but she wasn't the first president to break protocol.

Liz, who also floated beside Candy, admitted out loud, "It was me and my friends who blew you up at the press conference last week."

These could be her last words, so Liz felt she had to come clean. President Lundgrasse smiled at this and did little else to react. *Maybe she's thinking up some way to have me shipped to Siberia.* Finally, the president said, "Nice. I thought that was pretty funny, actually."

The virus Runsdeep jerked and contorted its torso like it was having a frenzied seizure. It looked down for the first time, straight down, and extended its hand in a gripping motion. Paula's body was instantly ripped from Candy's arms at tremendous speed by an unseen force. Once returned to the monster, Paula floated alongside it and started to twitch and contort just as Runsdeep did, and, when she stopped, her face had morphed into an ooze-covered, demonic corruption.

Materializing out of thin air, Terryl appeared on the opposite side of the virus and contorted himself in the same awful way, revealing his own twisted demon face. The squad and the rest of the taskforce braced themselves. Candy regained her composure momentarily, then was the first to break formation and dart at the sadistic nightmare that stood in the middle of the three.

The virus reacted in an instant. It had been waiting for this. Shooting its arms out in a domineering gesture, it commanded the possessed Paula and Terryl to fly out and meet Candy head on. Runsdeep flew straight up into the sky, widening the gap between itself and the fray. An impossible arsenal of world-ending powers were at her fingertips, but Candy still preferred taking pop-shots with her rocket launcher. She unleashed two screaming missiles at the virus before the puppets got in her way. Both missed as the rest of the team descended upon the battle. Half of them focused on Candy and the puppets while President Lundgrasse, the CEO, Liz, Eric, and a select Admin entourage pursued the big cheese. *Rank, putrid cheese,* Eric thought.

Possessed Paula's punches broke through the pain protection circuits in the Server programming just enough to make the intense thuds ache. The faint pain radiated up into Candy's throat. Tearfully she searched for a hint of Paula behind the puppet's villainous gaze, but received a kick to the skull in return, nearly putting her out of commission.

Waves of agents and government security personnel equipped with god-mode avatars took turns having their attacks parried and their bodies pummeled and propelled away like bullets from a gun. A few hit the ground in *DBZ* fashion with such force that they disappeared into the craters they formed, leaving them immobilized and stuck in the muddied code.

The battle ascended in dashes and leaps all the way up to the clouds, which obscured combat visuals so much that Candy lost sight of her target. The motion-tracking systems of the squad's suits kicked in, outlining the speeding form of the virus just in time to catch sight of the Terryl Puppet before it planted an elbow in Sam's face, temporarily putting xem out of action.

Maxx and all his maxed-out power came throwing punches. He traded blows with the dark specter of Terryl. The skin on his knuckles went dry, cracked and chilled after scraping at the goo-laden metallic frame that encased his opponent. Throwing his arm around Terryl in a headlock, Maxx discovered that not only was the dark matter sticking to the man's body unbearably cold, but now he couldn't let go of it. The puppet sped toward the ground in the mother of all suplexes, slamming Maxx into the earth with the force of a stock car crash.

Candy and Sam rendezvoused and descended to help but were punished by a swift upper cut from Terryl, again putting Sam out of the fray momentarily before clipping Candy, who grabbed the puppet as it went by, pushed off of it, and let fly a rocket that connected with the creature a scant ten yards away. The explosion blew back on Candy, but she survived thanks to her armor. Disoriented, the Terryl Puppet wobbled about erratically in the air. Unable to react in time, and with Candy and Sam stunned as well, Maxx called out to Eric over the general chat channel, "Incel Minor is dazed! Take him out!"

Eric had to help his friends, and the virus was getting away. Up until this point, he had been too afraid to attack, and now he wracked his brain for a course of action while Maxx called out again, "Admins, government goons, anybody! Help!"

Maxx felt the blood drain from his face when he saw the Paula Puppet zooming toward him. The agents and other taskforce soldiers that it defeated lay sprinkled across Prium's rooftops, and now it was making a beeline for him. Maxx dialed through the suit abilities and unleashed a force field that absorbed Paula's collision in the nick of time. Her attack was deflected, and the force field blipped audibly, then disappeared, rendered useless by the viral corruption.

Maxx cussed. He shouted at Sam, who was back in the air and ready to fight, "Terryl! Get Terryl!"

Sam darted toward the still-disoriented Terryl. Supported at last by Eric's barrage of missile fire, xe let fly a burst of god-mode energy. The resulting explosions blew every last drop of viral corruption free of the man's body, which appeared as a dark silhouette in a burst of teal light.

Sam called out xyr instructions over the general channel, telling everyone that they needed to disorient the virus with direct contact if they were ever going to slow it down long enough to get a clear shot. An oozy tentacle arm shot out of the Puppet Paula's back and interrupted xem. Bashed in the head and wrapped up in the awful, sticky appendage, Sam was completely immobilized. Paula reeled xem in. Subdued and afraid, Sam floated alongside the puppet while it took to attacking Maxx, Candy and Eric, who engaged the creature at the same time.

Destructive energy beams missed their targets. Physical blows were interwoven through the three-on-one fight in a ballet of violence. One after the other, tendrils and tentacles shot out from Paula's body and were ripped free by fiery angelic wrist-blades. Taking a chance, Maxx lunged for Paula's chest, but wound up tightly wrapped in a series of tendrils that he failed cut in time. Candy issued a bloodcurdling cry and hacked away at Paula's left side, exposing much of her original avatar's body, then Eric let fly a beam of code devastation that obliterated Paula's viral possessor.

Working quickly as they could, now that they could get close, Admins and agents seized Paula and Terryl's bodies to extract whatever remained of the hacked tethers wired into their brains. Doing this had an immediate effect on the entire Server.

Severing the pirated tethers triggered a cascade effect in

Runsdeep's network. The maelstrom's tendrils could now be seen to stretch all across the open fields outside of Prium, surrounding the city and threatening to infiltrate every program and subroutine that it contained. When he first noticed this scarring and penetration of the sky, the flame of hope went out inside Eric. These jagged lines, frozen lightning strikes coursing with the black ooze that had violated Candy's wife, were all over now, even reaching the ground and spreading into serrated rivers deltas. When the first tendrils hit the city wall, the stone programs moaned with the onset of corruption, and the virus Runsdeep cackled.

Seeing that Paula was regaining consciousness, Eric and Maxx flew up to meet the others, urging Sam to go with them, which xe did. The Admins and agents who had surrounded Paula to ascertain her health commanded her to log off immediately, then joined the mass of fighters pursuing the viral avatar. Paula rested in Candy's arms, exhausted, as though she had just run her longest marathon.

"Can we… get out of here now?" Paula asked, her face blank with fatigue.

Candy fought back tears hopelessly, "Yes, honey, yes we can!"

Reaching with both hands, Candy pulled off her own helmet while guiding Paula's hand to do so as well, and they disappeared in a shower of dissolving pixels.

Having reached nearly as high as it could go, Runsdeep finally stopped flying away from its pursuers and faced them. Storm clouds raged beneath them all. The dark avatar could hardly be seen against the infected sky. It had been daytime, but the virus' influence was corrupting even the weather programs now. The message it was sending was clear:

I do not come to bring peace or understanding. I come to cast out the light.

The first waves of Admins and Monitors shot forth in streams of varying patterns, all planned in advance under the direction of Mr. Military, but the virus decimated them in their dozens with a fierce machine gun's hail of metal darts. Morbidly riddled and torn to shreds, the poor Monitors' digital remains fell like party streamers to the ground. The Admins did not fare much better.

This slaughter can't go on, thought Eric, who joined the streams of Admins and called for them to rearrange their attack patterns. Well before coming within the range at which people were falling apart like loose yarn, Eric shot a burst of annihilation code in the form of a blue-white ball. The viral avatar sidestepped this like it was dodging a volleyball serve, and let fly a ribbon of cabled darts that pursued Eric like homing missiles.

While Eric worked hard to evade these doozies by cruising away as fast as he could, pitching in every direction as he flew along, Liz approached from behind and took her own shot, yielding the same result. Now they were both being chased by synchronized clouds of projectiles that moved like murderous migratory birds. Maxx saw where he was needed and picked off these nuisances one by one using both his annihilator cannon and his arm-blades.

The whole scene was a spectacle of carnage, bodies rent to shreds, screams of frustration and battle cries. Runsdeep moved with such speed that it forced its pursuers to collide with one another, and *its cackle-fit rang true not of a virus' behavior, but that of a man's,* Eric thought when at last he was free of the missiles.

"Thanks, Maxx!" Eric shouted with a nod. The two joined

each other in flight, then Liz and Sam found and joined them too. No one had gotten anywhere near the virus, nor had a single one of their blades or blasts. If god mode wasn't elite enough to handle this boss, what hope was there? Nobody said it. Everybody was thinking it. More gamer volunteers streamed up from the ground, having been granted the power of flight by the CEO. It was the Server against Runsdeep now, yet numbers seemed pointless. *What else can we do?* Looking at Sam, Eric saw the answer to his own question.

"Sam!" Eric shouted over to xem. Xe snapped to attention. "Steam-fish!"

Confused at first, Sam understood when Liz nudged xem and smirked. *Of course!*

Sam parted from the group and came at Runsdeep at a solitary angle. Noticing this from a mile away, the virus, or man, or whatever it was, broke away from the offense's weakened attacks and charged straight at Sam with blinding speed. Everyone watched in terror at the velocity of its movement. Liz and the squad felt their stomachs drop and squash into their bladders, a most horrible sinking at that sharp and sudden fear of losing Sam forever – true death, never to respawn.

Time then passed as it so often does when life is near its end, with Sam's sense of space and time slowing down, even here on the Server, and xe saw xyr life's fondest and most aggravating moments with xyr friends and family flash through xyr mind. Eric, Liz and the others all took varying angles to rush to xyr aid, but the blow was imminent. They were too late.

Verónica...

Just as xe had watched Candy do in her favorite game, Sam twisted with a snapping motion at the last millisecond, and the bull thought he was prepared for this. When xe dropped in

180

elevation, xe pivoted and grabbed hold of the thickest of tendrils xyr hand could clasp, piggybacking on the speeding monstrosity. The virus snarled and set itself a-spiraling in an attempt to remove Sam's grip. The blade-sharp edges of the virus-man's armor gouged and prodded at xem, and xe recoiled in alternating directions, agonized but maintaining xyr grip. They were getting close to the ground now after peeling through the cloud layer and pulling a great swathe of mist down with them. Eric and the squad were gaining on them. Runsdeep's growls were that of a crazed, rabid dog. Before it could sink its tendrils deep enough into Sam to hijack xyr nerve center and avatar, Sam let go and sailed straight up, slashing free of all gooey appendages that held xem.

The virus screeched in protest and doubled back after xem. On its way it was cut off by the squad, who fired a laser-wall of coding that ensnared it. The seeping corruption dried and cracked when the laser mesh struck it, and the virus wailed. Successive blasts of explosive coding were gobbed onto the elusive, oozing entity, anchoring it to the ground like a chain and immobilizing it at last.

Runsdeep thrashed like a varmint tied to a post. Admins swarmed the scene in an instant and erected a cube-shaped barrier that severed the far-reaching tendrils of the virus. The effect of this severing rocked the earth and sky. The frozen black lightening quivered and dissipated like carbonation. The virus-man wriggled, and the harder he fought, the more his corruption dwindled to reveal a weakened mechanical skeleton. The organic or AI thing was either in pain or successfully mimicking pain. Ash, taking it upon herself to do what she figured every CEO ought to, stepped up to deliver the final blow.

Charging this specially designed shot of code was going to take a few minutes, as the CEO had explained earlier. It was

181

essentially a package of eliminatory subroutines tailor-made to simultaneously boot the hacker or program while tracing its origins in RL.

"Everyone get back! This blast *will* crash the Server, and will hopefully obliterate the virus. I'm going to track the source code, so I should wake up at my desk with the final readout in front of me in a moment. Ms. President, should the worst happen and I become unresponsive, Admin One will take over the operation until I recover. Is that clear?"

Nobody could have missed her blaring over the general chat, and all were unnerved by her solemn words. It occurred to Eric then that the blast might result not only in the virus' obliteration, but in Lester's as well.

"Will the blast kill Lester if he's in there?" Eric asked the CEO. He urgently awaited her reply, but it did not come, and no one stepped forward to answer for her. Perhaps no one knew, Eric thought, or perhaps nobody was really concerned, considering all the damage that Runsdeep had done. Was it legal? The president had authorized any means necessary to take out the terrorist. It was authorized protocol to be sure, but there was something that nagged at Eric.

Time running out, Eric approached the anchored virus, its form a hissing gelatinous mass that swelled and bubbled like a pile of eggs frying in a pan. Beneath the melting outermost layer, Eric could see Lester's flesh, his face and neck, exposed to the virtual air, and he called out through the calamitous winds that encircled the virus,

"Lester! You have to let go. You don't have much time. The deconstructive program is too aggressive. It will kill you!"

The flesh trapped within the mechanical skeleton stirred only slightly. There was no telling whether he had actually heard

Eric's warning. Eric assumed he must have, unless the code's destructive effects were interfering with his audio signals. The deteriorating mass lurched, but no response came.

"You have one minute to log out and remove your virus," called the CEO, her arm cannon shaking with the power as it built up. Bursts of energy erupted from her arm and body in crackling arcs. Pops rivaling RL's loudest fireworks rocked the sound waves at random, underscored by the growing static background noise. The Server's data interpretation programs were beginning to fail. Forms held, but colors and finer details began to melt away like deviant water paints. There was a wobbling in the formerly steady structures of all things, with diagonal points oscillating back and forth, forming little undulations on every edge and contour.

Eric knew this was his last chance, "Think about everything you've ever experienced that was beautiful in life!" He paused, feeling hopeless, recalling all too well the sense of defeat that pervaded his every day before he learned how to live differently. Eric scoured his brain for more words. "Remember the way you felt when you first rode a bike; your earliest memories of ice cream and snow cones; that glow of the sunrise…"

"MOVE, NOW!" Ashley Fournier's entire body trembled with the power as it peaked in her arm cannon. She needed Eric to get out of the way or face annihilation along with the enemy. The blast was imminent.

Wretched creature, Lester arched his back and defiantly barked at the warnings he was given. He tore off the crusty metallic lining that covered his face and looked his destroyers in their eyes. Eric couldn't stomach it and darted toward the man to shout a final warning. A truck-sized column of electrical essence rendered the whole world silent, decimating code line after code line with its very passage through the non-air.

All players fell into the oblivion of logging off, backwards through the inky wells of computer language and smack dab into their seats at home. The CEO, Eric, and Lester remained while the universe descended into deluging waterfalls of program atoms that fell loose and free.

Eric's final shout muted, he turned to see the approaching light. He was no more than ten feet from Lester – well within the kill radius. The column waited for no one and connected with such finality and shock that for a moment, none of the three knew whether any of it had ever even existed.

Silence embraced Eric. He saw Lester a few paces away. The empty brightness obscured most of his body, but his face was visible. He was downcast, despondent, defeated, until he met Eric's eyes. If death were to take him in this moment, there was one thing that made Lester's whole rampage worth it – failure had shown him that the blackpill philosophy had worked out after all, at least it did now, in this moment. He could not change what he had done, what he had said, or whether he was about to die. His death was almost certain, and in the silent brightness, he was powerless to any chance at survival.

He let go. He let go of whatever might be or might have been.

Peace, if even for the briefest moment, was sweet.

Fifteen

Candy strutted her stuff like she was on the catwalk of a swanky Hollywood fashion show wearing the prized jewels of a foreign prince. Ditching the ferret body and dipping back into her own skin felt wonderful, even if it was virtual. Eric's transformation had inspired her. As he looked on unexpectedly and shyly aroused, she bounced her womanly assets around like she was cheering for NASCAR winners under a spray of champagne. Paula applauded.

The rooftop location at the center of Prium had been the best Ashley Fournier could muster. She offered every luxury free of charge. As far as the CEO was concerned, she was indebted to Liz and her squad. Candy took advantage of this and sampled a smorgasbord of cocktails, each with their own unique kick.

"Work it, girl!" Paula encouraged her to keep on dancing. Liz and Sam joined in the applause, hooting and hollering. Maxx smiled and raised a glass. Eric saw this and raised his glass too, outwardly having a very good time, while inwardly he still thought about Lester.

"Loud and proud, bitches!" Candy cried and raised a closed fist to cheers of agreement from even the agents in attendance who saw to any of the private party goers' questions or needs. This was to be the most elite of celebrations on the Server to date, and the CEO wanted to make sure that her guests of honor were thoroughly wined, dined, and rewarded.

The virus' eradication had led to the Server going offline for a four-day period. Maintenance was performed during this time. It was feared that the repairs would take months until, out of the blue, the damaged subroutines and programs were miraculously restored, as though by magic. Nobody was sure what to make of this exactly. Theories floated around of miscalculations of damage and the existence of an underlying, unseen niche where the virus awaited its next chance to strike.

"Want to dance, friend?" Candy flirtatiously offered a hand to help Eric up onto the table overlooking the cityscape that surrounded the rooftop patio. The afternoon skyline was a mosaic of watery jewels and glass walls. Paula knew Candy was just being extra friendly, but she wouldn't have been surprised if the drinks were making her forget her usual sexual orientation, and gave a combined shrug-smile when Eric looked to her.

"Have fun, kid!"

Eric gulped. Paula and Candy were probably a good ten years older than him.

"Oh, I won't get his hopes up," Candy insisted as he got onto the table with her and started to dance, playfully mimicking her twerk style. "You'll meet the right lady someday. Don't worry, Eric!"

The squad collectively cringed. They knew it was a sensitive topic for him. At least now they did. But Eric didn't cringe. He didn't sulk, and he didn't get upset. He kept on dancing, and he smiled back at them all. Sure, he'd meet the right lady someday, but what was the rush? There was no rush. Rushing things, he had learned, could be bad, and some things you just do not rush, like your death. Or orgasms. At least Liz said as much, to the friendly laughter of all. Eric laughed too, and kept on dancing.

Liz noticed Maxx had trailed off from the group after a string of jokes and more laughter. He did this from time to time. It couldn't be helped. He was a broody man on the best of days, and everyone knew he was still in mourning. She would let him have his alone time, but not just yet.

"Impressive work out there, as usual," Liz said and rested her elbows against the clear railing just as Maxx did. He regarded her warmly but briefly, then looked back to the artificial horizon, cloudless and colorful.

"What's eating you?"

Maxx started to speak then stopped twice. Almost giving up, he pushed the words out, "What kind of messed up planet is this if people like Lester can screw with society? You heard about the technology the government types said they found. The dude is some kind of super genius, so if he wants to lay low and strike again, there's nothing anyone can do."

Liz could tell this was bothering him a lot, and tried to reassure him. "They'll be looking for him, and security is being tightened. I guess if we don't feel safe we could just stay offline…"

"No, see, but then he wins. And that's what's really pissing me off about it all," Maxx looked back at the rest of the gang, dancing and drinking still, clueless as to his internal drama. "It's that I have to live in fear. My friends have to live in fear. And women most of all, women who are the common targets…"

When Maxx got angry, it didn't matter how rationally or irrationally he was thinking. It was hard for him to calm down.

"That's the world, isn't it?" Liz offered meekly.

"What?"

"Danger. Risk of death. The way it can all suddenly end. It's cruel." Liz looked back at her friends now too. She smiled upon seeing them all smile. "We've got to laugh at the ridiculous, unforgiving universe." Liz was never one for poetics, but when it came to helping her dear friend, she reached for a way. "I don't know if the world will ever be rid of people like him. People suffer... and sometimes they don't react well to the suffering, whether completely by their own choice or not."

Maxx wanted to tear this argument to pieces because it sounded so backwards, but he stopped himself. Maybe there was more to the reality of the situation than he could appreciate. He sighed, and began to let go. People who harm the innocent, as Liz tells it, were like vipers in the swamp – hazards that would crop up in the world. Human minds were more complex than that, however, and he knew this. He decided they'd have a good long talk about it later that night over more drinks. Satisfied, Maxx and Liz returned to the party. Sam cheered on two agents, one awkward and one thrilled, as they lined up Jell-O shots on Candy's stomach, which Paula hungrily devoured.

Later that night, Sam had logged off and was sitting alone in xyr apartment. Tired of first-person mode, xe flipped on the television. The news was on, and the TV anchor introduced a live feed of a speech that was being given by CEO Ashley Quinn Fournier. Sam turned up the volume.

... all in order at a later juncture. Yes, that's true, Ryan, and I have apologized for that. I hope now that we can move on with the future of the VirtuaHelm^{TM} and its implications for society at large. All new technologies experience bumps in the road, Ryan, and this is no different. The first steam trains used to explode, historical casualties in mining accidents alone can reach numbers that bring the hardest of us to tears, and this recent breach in Server security will be a much more short-lived blip in comparison. Between contracts with the military for aerial, submarine, and land-based operations, limited universal public

use through the national library system, coordination with travel agencies and NASA – the list is long! This much is sure, Ryan, the future looks bri–

Sam turned the TV off and sank back into xyr couch. With no one around to hear xem, xe said to xemself contently, "Today was a good day."

CEO Ashley Fournier let herself fall onto the imperial bed laden with satin. The speech she'd given had exhausted her, like all public appearances, and with no more company business to attend to for the day, she could slip off her shoes and melt into a pile of luxury pillows. There she would remain until a thirst for something to smooth out all the edges reminded her that there were plenty of selections on the wine rack.

An aged Bordeaux, the thirst ordered her, and, reluctantly rising from the bed a final time, she obeyed. She busted out her best crystal with etched walls that tapered to the thinnest of rims, recalling how it felt to use them – as if one were sipping wine that flowed forth from the air.

Bottle opener in hand, she set to work. There would be an onslaught of international pressure on her now. Not that this wasn't typically the case, but now, with a whole new frontier stretched out before the people of Earth, and as its pioneer, she had to answer for it. Critics said that no amount of PR campaigning would make up for the damage the hacker had done to the company image. The educational departments of several countries immediately revoked their bids to participate in an experimental school which could be attended by anyone with an Internet connection. She felt confident that her friends in government would help her bring them back around, but there were no guarantees. After pouring one heavy glass for herself, she poured a second and brought it over to her new best friend in the government, who waited on the bed in her sexiest black lingerie.

"*Thank* you, darling," President Lundgrasse said, delighted, "and thank you for having me over."

"Well, thank *you* for accepting my invitation to meet tonight." Ashley admired the magnificently delicious woman, "You won't get into any trouble for being gone this long from the White House? I thought you were shackled there until the end of your term."

"Nope. It turns out that's not a thing. As long as I stay out of trouble, they can't tell me anything. Plus, I'm not breaching any expectations of decency since I'm not married. You worry too much."

Ashley shook with an unexpected trill of laughter, "Man, I was *freaked the fuck out* when that secret security agent walked up to my window before my limo driver pulled away from the company building."

"Ah, yes. That one. He's basically a ninja." The president took a sip from her glass and watched the changing shades of twilight.

Ashley sighed, snuggled up closer to the POTUS, and spoke in as soft and sexy a voice as possible, "I was surprised when they told me that you accepted the invitation."

"What, because of our little spat in the conference room? A gal needs moxie to be president. And they're coming at me extra hard now too. The stack of bills to have your company's technology made illegal is going to be nauseating, even if most of them are doomed nonstarters."

"Um, hello! I didn't think you'd accept because of your Supreme Court picks and all the Bible stuff, you nitwit!" Ash caressed her thigh in exactly the right way, just as she'd done earlier.

Yessica faltered, a deer caught in the lights.

"What can I say? Don't judge a book by its cover."

Ashley took Yessica's hand in her own and traced the edges of her fingertips, "Can you help me track down the hacker and pump up my cyber security?"

Yessica frowned. Ashley was a persuasive businesswoman, and that would get her almost everywhere tonight – almost – but if she was going to provide Ashley and her company with government support in her quest for a safer VR Server, she would need congressional approval, and she told her that. There were only so many power plays she could pull before she got herself labelled as a tyrant with a target on her back. That didn't mean there wasn't anything she could do for Ashley, though. Yessica snuck one last sip of wine before setting her glass down and focusing all her attention on helping Ms. CEO relax.

The glow of keyboards and six separate computer towers changed color constantly and in sync. It was a setup fitting for a gamer of a certain variety – clinical and organized. The occupant of the space would have once described it as a hideout, but the curtains were coming down. One, then another. Light was making its way in. All metaphorically of course. Even if his upstairs room at his mom's house were on fire, Lester wouldn't ever take down his black-out curtains. No, it was another kind of light.

Lester decided that it wouldn't be worth dying for a cause that had made him miserable for longer than he cared to remember. Logging out at the last second, the shell that was his avatar perished, but he escaped by the slimmest slice of a second. Once free of the Server, he knew that they'd never be able to trace his coding. What's more, the tips of the tendrils and tentacles he'd sent out into the virtual world had left pinpoints of contagion that acted as antennae and seeds for a potential future virus. He could raise an army of Runsdeep AI soldiers if he wanted to. They would have to destroy the computer servers or physically sever them from the network to stop him.

The viral tendrils had caused enormous damage to Server infrastructure, but all of this was reversed, and the security even improved when Lester entered the command to remove all hacked uploads and infiltrations. It was a great unraveling that he had neither planned nor designed. No – driven and inspired by a second chance, he manually sculpted every piece of the command and consciously repaired every path of destruction like he was sewing a rip in his jacket.

As he sorted through the twisted strands of code from a safe distance, untraceable to existing Server technology while working in RL, Lester recalled those golden memories that Eric had urged him to remember: the sound of his older brother's laugh before he tragically died young; the arriving autumnal winds that tugged at him as he walked across clearings and fields; the smiling face of his childhood best friend when they caught a fish together using a homemade fishing pole fashioned out of a stick. He laid another fold of Server coding against its severed counterpart and repaired it. Another fold of coding repaired, another fold of his heart mended.

On January 19th of the year 2052, Lester wanted to live.

THE END

Milton Keynes UK
Ingram Content Group UK Ltd.
UKHW010823141223
434360UK00001B/36